FOR HAILE AND YARA AND
AYA AND MAKAI AND ZENAI

TABLE OF CONTENTS

DANIEL JOSÉ OLDER

DACTYL HILL SQUAD

➤ BOOK THREE ➤
THUNDER RUN

SCHOLASTIC PRESS • NEW YORK

Library of Congress Cataloging-in-Publication Data available
ISBN 978-1-338-26887-4

10 9 8 7 6 5 4 3 2 1   20 21 22 23 24

Printed in the U.S.A.   23
First edition, June 2020

Book design by Christopher Stengel

· PART ONE ·

ATCHAFALAYA

CHAPTER ONE
TOAD, TOAD, TOAD

FOR A FEW moments, a strange quiet settled over the Atchafalaya Swamplands. Magdalys Roca, standing on top of a gigantic toad, looked over to her brother, Montez, whom she'd traveled all the way from New York City to rescue. He stared back at her from the shattered fifth-floor window of a dilapidated mansion; peeling pink shutters dangled off rusty hinges on either side. He carried a sighted rifle, the kind the sharpshooters used, and that made sense: He'd become a soldier in these past couple months of war, a sniper. He'd taken lives, and now, so had Magdalys. And she was a soldier now, just like him.

"Um," Corporal Wolfgang Hands said from a window a few floors down. He was a big man with a dashing mustache, light brown skin, and a black eye patch. He'd gotten his men to the safety of this swamp mansion after their medical convoy had been ambushed, and this was where Magdalys and her friend Mapper had found them, hemmed in by Confederate Bog Marauders with more on the way. Magdalys had sent the enemy scattering when she'd brought her giant toad crashing down from across the lake. But she could already hear the rustle and yells of the swampland guerrilla soldiers regrouping. "You do know how to control that thing, don't you, young lady?"

"Sure seems like she does," someone yelled. "Unless it just happened to take her to us and scatter the Marauders."

"The other two are still giving 'em a good lickin' out on the lake," a young soldier with a nasty scar down the center of his face pointed out. The others scoffed and rolled their eyes. "No pun intended!"

Magdalys smirked. Last time she'd looked, the two toads behind them had been lashing out at an attacking brigade of mounted sinornithosaurs with their humongous tongues, swallowing a few and knocking others out of the sky in wild spirals. She looked Corporal Hands dead in the eye. "I do control these toads, sir," she said. "My name is Magdalys Roca and I'm the greatest dinowrangler in the world."

"And I'm Mapper!" Mapper said. "I mean, I'm Kyle, but they call me Mapper."

"Wait, you wrangle dinos?" Montez said.

"Wait, as in the famous Magdalys Roca that Razorclaw over here won't shut up about?" Corporal Hands said.

"Wait, as in the Magdalys Roca who I sent that dactyl-gram?" another soldier yelled.

Magdalys gaped at him. That gram — the matrons of the Colored Orphan Asylum had given it to her the night of the Draft Riots back in July; the night everything changed. "Private Tom Summers?"

He nodded. "The same! Glad you made it! But I didn't mean for —"

"Enough chitter chatter!" the corporal hollered. "Those Bog Marauders'll be back here any minute, and remember, with only one bite from one of their sinosteeds you'll be —"

"Dying slowly in a pool of your own vomit and drool," the other five soldiers all groaned at once.

"We remember," Montez said. Then he hoisted his rifle up, squinted through the sight, and let off a shot that Magdalys heard whiz past her and then land with a distant juicy thunk. She whirled around as the caw of a sinornith rang out, saw it plummeting from the sky, its rider already splashing into the lake below with a yelp.

"Whoa!" She looked back at her brother, blinking. "You really are a crack shot."

"Time to go," Montez said. "They're almost here." He disappeared from the window, gathering his things, and Magdalys had to remind herself he was still that goofy kid who loved reading and looked out for everyone at the orphanage. Kind of.

JUH!! the huge toad beneath her boomed. It was a

guttural, raspy chirp that only Magdalys could hear, or feel really, as it seemed to rise like a tiny marvelous earthquake from within her. And she understood it, this ancient creature's strange one-sound language — he was ready to go too, and he wouldn't wait long. Behind her, two of the dactyls they'd flown into the swamplands, Beans and Dizz, huddled protectively over the third, Grappler, who'd been wounded just before they found the toads.

Come! Magdalys sent her thought arcing to the lake behind them, felt it reach the other two toads, felt their attention turn suddenly toward her. *Come!*

"Brace yourself," she said to Mapper, and then the whole planet seemed to rock with the sudden explosive landing of a toad on one side of them, and then again as the second one landed on the other side.

"Yeeesh!" Mapper yelled, steadying himself.

Magdalys wiggled her eyebrows at him. "I warned ya!"

He shook his head. "What happens now?" Mapper had been with her all the way from New York — in fact, he was the only one left of the tight-knit squad they'd formed back in Brooklyn. Two Step and Sabeen had been swept up in the Battle of Chickamauga and were probably holed up in Chattanooga with their new friend Hannibal and the rest of the Army of the Cumberland, surrounded by Confederates and anxiously awaiting General Grant to help them escape. Cymbeline Crunk, one of the greatest Shakespearean actresses ever (as far as Magdalys was concerned, anyway) and a Union spy, had flown to Tennessee with General Grant on the back of Stella, the giant pteranodon that Magdalys had saved from a silo back in Dactyl Hill. And Amaya was headed west to find her father, an eccentric general in the US Army, and figure out the riddle of her Apache mother.

Kwa-THOOM!! A mortar shell hurtled through the top tower of the mansion, obliterating it and showering Magdalys and Mapper with debris and broken glass. She glanced at the window Montez had been in just as he poked his big toothy grin out of it and waved. "I'm alright!"

"Let's move out!" Corporal Hands yelled.

Magdalys exhaled. Just like that, after all that . . . her brother could've been killed. Could still be killed.

She narrowed her eyes at the approaching sinornithosaurs as the corporal barked orders. "Summers and Bijoux, take the toad on the left! Toussaint and Briggs, the right!"

At some point along the way, the journey had stopped being just about saving Montez, and become something much bigger inside Magdalys. *The Union needed her*, generals kept saying. With her abilities, she could crush the Confederacy. And she knew it was true.

"Aye, aye, sir!" The men called as the magnificent toads lowered themselves toward the windows.

She'd seen firsthand how being able to get inside the minds of dinosaurs could sway the tide of battle. And she'd seen what could happen when agents of the Knights of the Golden Circle, a secret society trying to build a slavery-driven empire all throughout the Americas, had used it to their own ends. In fact, she'd seen it less than an hour ago, when Earl Shamus Dawson Drek, a Bog Marauder who had the same power she did, had bombarded her with swarms of dinos. She'd bested him, breaking through the lock he had on those reptilian minds to divert the attacks away from her and Mapper, but it took everything she had. And Drek was still out there.

She knew they had to be stopped. She knew she was one of the few who might be able to do it. So she'd agreed to join the US Army.

But it wasn't the Union she cared about, not really.

"Roca," Corporal Hands called, "you and I will hop on with your sister here."

Montez nodded and, as bullets whistled through the air around them, climbed out the window and leapt onto the snout of the toad.

Her brother. She watched him make his way up toward her. Yes, it was still for him that she'd done this, but now it was for all her brothers, and her sisters too. She thought about the plantations they'd flown over as they approached the Atchafalaya, the scars etched across her friend Big Jack Jackson's back. No one she loved would be safe until the Confederacy fell and the Knights of the Golden Circle were defeated forever.

Montez slipped and let out a grunt as he scrambled for purchase — that hide was slippery with slime and swamp water, but the warts and folds allowed for easy footholds. A few more shots rang out but whizzed harmlessly past. Montez pulled himself to his feet, and then made it to the top and wrapped Magdalys in a quick hug as Corporal Hands grumbled and stumbled his way out the window and toward them.

She had an army at her back now. And General Grant had given her the command of her own special elite unit of dinowarriors, had even put it in writing. She could hunt down the Knights and take apart their organization piece by piece.

"Thanks for rescuing me," Montez whispered.

She punched his shoulder. "Anytime, big bro."

And taking apart the Knights was exactly what she planned to do.

She turned to the lake behind them, and the toad waddled from one side to the other, turning too.

"Whoa! Whoa!" Wolfgang yelled, his hands stretched out to either side for balance as he made his way up to them. "Gotta warn us when he gonna do that, young lady!" He scurried to the spot between the toad's eyes where Magdalys, Mapper, and Montez stood prepping their weapons. Out over the lake, the sinornith riders yelped and let off a volley of musket fire.

But before Magdalys could take apart any evil organizations, she'd have to get out of this mess.

"Get ready," she yelled. The three soldiers around her raised their weapons. Off to either side, Toussaint, Briggs, Summers, and Bijoux did the same.

JUH!!! the toad burped urgently, lowering itself. Then it hurtled out over the lake amidst the crackle of gunfire.

"ATTACK!!"

CHAPTER TWO
LAKESIDE SKIRMISH

THEY CAME CRASHING down at the far edge of the lake with a tremendous *fwa-SHOOOOOM!!* And a wall of water blasted up on either side of them. Magdalys was pretty sure they'd taken out a few sinorniths on their way down, but a bunch of others were cascading toward them from nearby treetops, their riders howling with glee.

Montez and Mapper were on their feet first, and they'd each taken two shots when a shadow covered the approaching Bog Marauders. The Confederates looked up and their howls turned to screeches and then were cut off entirely when the gigantic toad blitzed out of the sky on top of them and landed with a *kaFOOOM!!*

JuhJuhJuhJUH! the toad chortled beneath Magdalys.

SHASHOOM!!! came the splash announcing that the third toad had landed on their other side.

More sinornith riders were coming though, and they seemed to be closing in from all around.

"How many of these guys are there?" Mapper grunted. He let off shot after shot at the approaching swarm with his carbine, but Magdalys couldn't tell if he was hitting any of them. A few bullets zinged past, none too close.

"They've been pestering us since we holed up about a week ago," Wolfgang explained. "First it was just a few, but they musta sent word out and more and more started gathering." *BLAM!!* He had a pistol in each hand and shot one and then the other. *BLAM!!*

The sinorniths glided toward the treetops up ahead, probably so their riders could take more accurate potshots.

"Corporal!" Summers called from the toad to their right. "Private Bijoux has been hit!"

"Crikey," Wolfgang muttered.

"Ju-ju-just a flesh wound, sir!" Bijoux yelled. "I'm alright!"

The sinoriders dismounted amidst the canopy of live oaks and cypress trees, and then their steeds immediately launched back into the blue skies. They were ugly creatures, with gray-brown feathers, thick hind legs, and narrow necks leading to those fierce raptor-like jaws, which would deliver a deadly dose of venom to anyone they grasped. And they were swooping toward Magdalys and the others with a clamor of squeaks and caws.

Earl Shamus Dawson Drek. Magdalys narrowed her eyes. It had to be him. He'd survived the toad attacks, had probably been hiding in the underbrush all along, biding his time, and now, wherever he was, he had a whole squad of sinorniths at his command.

"Take aim, lads!" Wolfgang commanded. "But we don't have much ammo to waste, so wait till you have a shot before you fire."

And it was one thing to fend off attacks against her and one other person, but seven other people, spread out over three toads? Maybe one day, but she wasn't there yet.

But Drek . . . if she could get to Drek . . .

"Can you and your men hold them off for a few minutes, Corporal Hands?" Magdalys asked, trying to get the sharp, clipped military tone right.

"Fire, boys! Give 'em everything you got!" He looked down at her as gunfire erupted around them, gave a kind of sideways tilt with the top of his head. "I think we can handle 'em for a bit. Don't be long though. I already have a wounded soldier and we're all in desperate need of a bath."

"Yes, sir!" Magdalys said, snapping off a salute as best she could. "Can I also borrow my brother for this mission?" She was already backing toward where the dactyls were huddled.

"Alright, but make it quick!" Wolfgang nodded at Montez, who let off two more shots, then stood and followed Magdalys.

"Great," she said. "Just try not to hit us while you're at it."

"Hit you? But . . ."

"Dizz!" Magdalys yelled, breaking into a run, and the tall purple pterodactyl perked his head up and blinked. "Let's go." Dizz nuzzled Grappler once more and then hopped twice toward Magdalys. She wrapped her arms around his neck and heaved herself onto his saddle; Montez leapt up behind her and with two powerful flaps, they soared out into the sky.

"How did you, ah, get a handle on dinos so fast?" Montez asked over the whipping wind and gunfire. "Our guy Toussaint is the best wrangler in the 9th and he's been training his whole life."

"It's . . . it's hard to explain," Magdalys said. She had promised her friend Redd that she wouldn't half step anymore in talking about her powers, and she'd been pretty good at it so far, but somehow . . . telling her brother that she could communicate with dinos using her mind just seemed impossible. "But I will! Once we're out of this mess. Can you handle yourself with a dactyl?"

She veered them in a wide circle and then sent Dizz careening toward the attacking sinorniths.

Fubbafubbafubba fooooooo came Dizz's jubilant war cry.

"I'm pretty decent," Montez said.

"Good," Magdalys said. She pulled Dizz into a sharp climb over the sinorniths, then leveled out and carefully stood up in the saddle.

"Why?" Montez asked. "What're you — AAAH!!"

Magdalys leapt.

CHAPTER THREE
SINORNITH SWOOP

THE WIND WHOOSHED through her, screamed against her face. Directly below, the brown-green murk of the swamplands awaited, but there was a whole swarm of gliding dinos between her and the ground, all she had to do was pick one and . . .

With a squawking clamor that knocked the wind out of her, Magdalys landed on the back of a swooping sinornithosaurus and hugged tight to his neck as they both went plummeting toward the swamps.

"Mags!" Montez called from above.

Up, Magdalys thought, as hard as she could. But Drek's hold on this one was tight — her pleas seemed to crash against that empty feeling she'd come to understand as being blocked by another dinowarrior. *Up!* she urged. *Come on, boy!*

The sinornith plummeted at an even sharper angle, then craned his long neck around and snapped at Magdalys. She pulled her hands away just in time, then glared directly into those wild reptilian eyes. "You're mine now," she yelled, "so behave yourself!"

Just inches above a pool of murky swamp water, the sinornith pulled himself into a glide, landed briefly on a branch, and then launched back skyward as Magdalys let out a woot. It was strange, clutching all those swamp-slicked feathers and that thick neck; she'd gotten used to the dactyls' mostly bare hides. And sinorniths didn't fly exactly — they hurtled into the air and then glided along toward the ground. It would take some getting used to. *Feeeshwahh!* the dino cawed into her mind. He had been under Drek's control all morning and was bleary-minded, confused. She would try to keep a looser rein on him than what the Confederate dinomaster must've had.

"Montez!" she called. "Follow me!"

It took him a few tries, but he finally managed to get Dizz into a semigraceful flutter toward the tree line that Magdalys and her new steed had landed on and then taken off from again.

"Whaaaat was tha — AAAAHH!" Montez tried to ask, but Dizz decided to do a loop-de-loop while he was talking.

"Dizz!" Magdalys stifled a giggle. "Be nice. That's my brother."

The dactyl righted himself and bobbed his head from side to side with a soft squawk.

"They really do listen to you," Montez said.

You have no idea, Magdalys thought with a smile. "Keep me covered for a sec, okay? I have to do something."

Montez nodded and unslung his sniper rifle.

Okay, buddy, Magdalys thought, scanning the trees below. *Where was that guy who was controlling you before, hm?*

They'd circled around again and were heading back toward the others, keeping close to the edge of the lake. Drek would have to be somewhere where he could easily see what was going on. Probably in the underbrush nearby.

Feeshwaahh! the sinornith wailed, then it let out a screech and dove. The swampy lake water swung up toward Magdalys and for a second she thought they'd splash right into it. Instead, they skimmed along the top, sending ripples and tiny splashes to either side, then banked sharply back to the shore, where the sinornith touched down long enough for a quick, bumpy run through the mud before taking back off.

Dactyls were more fun and easier to ride, Magdalys decided, trying to keep track of the spinning landscape around her. Plus they didn't kill you with one bite. They'd branch-hopped back toward the upper canopy and now swooped over the treetops once again and . . . there! A gray-clad figure with bright red hair stood amidst the treetops, gazing at the shoot-out through a spyglass.

Magdalys glared, tilting her sinornith slightly so their dive would take them in right behind Drek. They swung toward him. The wind rose to a shrill howl. If she could snatch him up before he had a chance to fight back, they could bring him to New Orleans and interrogate him, find out where the other Knights of the Golden Circle in the area were hiding out, then hunt them down and capture them, one by one. They could dismantle the whole — The sinornith let out a shriek.

Drek spun around, yelled.

She was close enough to make out the splotches of mud on his uniform, that long red beard, the gold cap on one of his teeth, even. But not close enough to snatch him up, especially not now that he'd seen them. Drek pulled a pistol out of his belt and aimed it directly at Magdalys. She crouched low against the sinornith's filthy back as the first shot rang out, then another bang came from behind her. Magdalys peered up from her crouch; she saw Drek yell and clutch his hand, the pistol nowhere to be seen. He glanced at Magdalys with an enraged snarl and then disappeared into the trees just as she came swooping to a landing where he had been seconds earlier.

Out in the sky, Montez approached on Dizz, still flapping in odd, lopsided loops. He had his rifle out but was clearly having trouble holding on to it and not falling to his death from the wild dactyl. Over by the lake, the remaining sinorniths were flapping away now that Drek had stopped controlling them.

"Quite a shot," Magdalys called as Montez got closer.

"Hardly." He shrugged. "I was aiming for his head."

Inside, Magdalys flinched ever so slightly. She still wasn't totally used to this wartime world, where taking lives had become second nature, a simple act of survival. Even though Drek was about to kill her, had tried, and would again, it was jarring to think Montez was so ready to destroy him. But of course he was! They were enemies. At war.

She studied her brother as Dizz landed on the branch beside her and the sinornith. Had he gotten taller in the few months since she'd seen him? Would that sadness she now saw in his eyes ever go away? "You saved my life," she said.

He scoffed. "You saved all our lives by showing up, Mags."

She shook her head but didn't know why. It seemed wrong to accept that somehow. Everyone had put themselves in danger. The world had become indecipherably tangled, a web of people who had saved and killed one another, life debts and blood rivalries on into forever. "I'm going after him. We can't let Drek get away."

Montez squinted at her, taking her in now the way she had him a moment earlier. For a second, she thought he was going to pull an older brother I-can't-let-you-put-yourself-in-danger type move, which would've been laughable, considering where they were and what they'd both been through. Instead, he nodded. "We have a lot to talk about, huh, Mags?"

"We do indeed."

He pulled on the reins and spurred Dizz into the air. "I'll get the others."

CHAPTER FOUR
PURSUIT THROUGH THE SWAMP TREES

THE WOODS BUZZED and hummed and chirped and growled around Magdalys. It was so alive! The most living, breathing place she'd ever been. The sinornith stood perched on a branch far above the forest floor. They'd followed Drek to a relatively dry area just outside the Atchafalaya. Everything was muddy brown and green, and huge bugs flitted through the thick air amidst swarms of tiny flies.

Drek was nowhere to be seen.

She heard her brother calling out to the others, and, somewhere closer, the mournful hooting of a swamp owl. A fluttering of wings. The ongoing swoosh and splish of water all around.

No Drek.

She closed her eyes and opened up the part of herself that tuned in with dinominds. A whole world of chatter unfolded, like a curtain drawn to reveal a play midscene: the gentle, snorting mutter of the sinornith beneath her, the steady *juhjuhjuh* of the toads beneath it all, a squeaking pack of microdactyls nearby, and . . . there! Somewhere up ahead, a large, ferocious dino was tearing through the underbrush. It was already too far for her to reach to control and getting farther by the second.

Her eyes sprang open. "Heeyah!" she called, spurring the sinornith into a spiraling descent from one tree branch to another. The only direction was forward. They snapped through the dangling vines and Spanish moss, dipped around a huge oak tree, and then seemed to ricochet off another and blast deeper into the thick forest.

Finally, with her heart pounding in her ears and her face burning from scratches and cuts, Magdalys pulled her sinornith to a halt on a branch a few feet above the ground and listened. Again, the screeches and caws rose out of the forest around her, but the giant lizard she'd sensed moving away quickly: gone. And probably Drek with it.

She clenched her teeth and spurred her mount into a low glide. He was getting tired; she could feel the fast rise and fall of his breath beneath her, the gradually spreading slowness of his reactions. They dipped and dove forward, then up, then branch-to-branched it for a while until the sinornith started to cough and sputter.

"Alright, boy, alright," Magdalys said, taking him down for a landing. Catching her breath, the sound came to her again. It was unmistakable: a snorting, heaving, thrashing, snarling. It wasn't too far now, whatever it was. Somehow, she'd almost caught up.

She stretched outward with her mind, trying to grasp hold of the creature's sense, but it didn't take. The thing was either too far or too much within Drek's grasp for her to reach.

The sinornith panted beside her, still recovering. She'd have to go on foot until she could wrangle up another dino to ride. "One last favor," she said, running her hand along the creature's slick feathers. "Then I'll leave you alone."

Up, she thought as she jogged off through the trees. *Up, up, up.*

Behind her, the tired sinornith heaved itself from one branch to the next toward the sky.

"Okay," Magdalys said as her boot disappeared into the ground with a slurpy, bubbly noise. "This was a terrible idea. I get it!" She found a less mushy place to anchor her other foot and then yanked herself free, wobbled once, flapped her arms like a dactyl, and managed to stay upright. "A terrible, terrible idea!"

She kept going, now more carefully. The whole forest seemed to be turning into mud around her. On either side, greenish pools reflected glints of sunlight back toward the treetops. Gnats fussed and buzzed everywhere.

It hadn't all been for nothing, though. When Magdalys was quiet, she could still feel the gnashing tingle of that dino up ahead. Drek's mount, she was sure of it.

She gritted her teeth and pushed forward, hopping over another puddle and then sliding knee deep into the muck where she'd landed. "Gah!" She trudged out, soaked, each move she made a whole mess of squishiness and swamp water. Leaned against a tree and caught her breath.

She was about to close her eyes to try to find Drek again when she realized she didn't have to. *Fakatika fakatika fakatika fakatika* came the panting snarl of an approaching dino. It sounded like it might be laughing. And then the whole swamp seemed to erupt as heavy stomps crashed toward her.

Magdalys pulled out her carbine just as a towering spinosaur shoved its way through the underbrush. Drek straddled the part of its back where that sharp sail connected to its neck. He clutched the reins in one hand and his pistol in the other. Had he seen her?

She reached out with her mind. If she could get inside that thing's thoughts, she'd be able to — The spinosaur's alligator-like face snapped in her direction, wide green eyes locking with hers. It wasn't in her control though, not by a long shot. The dino lunged toward her.

Magdalys raised the carbine, tried to steady it, and squeezed the trigger. The shot went wide, and Drek answered with two shots of his own that whizzed through the clearing smoke around Magdalys and thunked into the tree she'd been leaning up against.

Time to go.

She dipped around to the other side of the tree and ran, ignoring the sucking, sinking mud beneath her boots and the sogginess of her trousers.

Another shot cracked the branches above her head, and the spinosaur let out a chilling roar from that long, toothy snout and plodded after Magdalys.

From somewhere behind them, a huge crash rumbled through the forest, then another. That would be the toads landing where she'd sent her sinornith up into the air to alert them to where she was, Magdalys thought. The third one landed with a splash and the scattered squawking of microraptors.

Were they too late though? How far had Magdalys wandered in this ridiculous chase?

JuhjuhjuhJUHjuhjuhJUH, the toads sang inside Magdalys.

She ran, praying her desperation would carry to them somehow, become a beacon. She definitely didn't have it in her to concentrate on reaching out.

BLAM! Blam BLAM! Drek's pistol screamed behind her, and bullets plunked into the marsh on either side, one kapinging off a rock and then thwunking into a log. The spinosaur roared and crashed through branches. But it sounded like he was farther away now. She glanced back. Drek had turned, sent his mount galloping off to the side, away from Magdalys. She squinted after him. Where were they going?

JuhJUHjuhjuhJUHjuhJUHjuhJUHJUHjuh.

At least now she had backup, she thought, taking a few careful steps after him, carbine still out. The crash of the toads moving through the forest rose up behind her. And then yells filled the air. She thought it might've been Montez's voice. And Wolfgang's. Then a round of gunshots burst out from up ahead.

What was happening?

JuhJUHjuhJUHJUHJUHJUHJUHJUH.

Magdalys broke into a run, although she had no idea which way to go. Up above, a familiar caw sounded: Dizz. She caught a flash of his purple hide sailing past the trees overhead. More gunfire. *Lots* of gunfire, and then the shriek of mortar shells cutting through the air.

BorGOOP! a toad moaned out loud as the artillery fire exploded.

"Mags!" a familiar voice yelled. Twigs snapped up above, and there was Mapper on top of Dizz, blasting through the forest toward her. "Hop on! We gotta get outta here!"

She did, grabbing hold of the saddle as Dizz slowed to a glide beside her and heaving herself on behind Mapper. And then they soared up, up, up, through the trees and above the canopy, into the sky. "What happened?" Magdalys asked.

And then she saw it. "Oh."

Another shell whistled through the air. In a clearing up

ahead, several divisions of gray-clad Confederate soldiers on spinoback unleashed a barrage of musket fire at the three toads, who peered down from the treetops. These soldiers weren't the ragtag local militias; they stood in military formation and looked to be well supplied and ready for war. A mounted artillery division of stegos lined up at the edge of the woods, letting off one shot after another from their howitzers.

"We found the enemy," Mapper said. "Like, all of them."

CHAPTER FIVE
ESCAPE

THEY'D SCRAMBLED AWAY as fast as they could. The Confederates had lobbed a couple more artillery shells after them and sent a few squads out, but the pursuit had seemed to fall away almost immediately. That relieved Magdalys, who was exhausted from chasing Drek in circles through the swamplands, but Wolfgang grunted that it was probably a bad sign and wouldn't elaborate when the others pressed him.

"March," he'd said gruffly. "Double time."

And they'd headed off into the wilderness.

A chorus of buzzing insect songs rose in the darkening sky over the Atchafalaya. Privates Toussaint and Briggs headed up the march, muskets out, bayonets fixed. Montez, Magdalys, Wolfgang, and Mapper walked alongside each other in the middle, and Tom Summers and Louis Bijoux, whose left arm had been grazed by some shrapnel but was otherwise okay, took up the rear.

The toads weren't far. Magdalys could feel the endless, curmudgeonly enthusiasm of their *juhJUH*s chortling on and on from somewhere off to the left. They were probably mostly submerged in a nearby lagoon, tending to each other's wounds and gossiping about the tiny mammals they'd just encountered. She had a feeling they wouldn't stray far though; they seemed to regard her and her friends as their responsibilities — or pets maybe. Anyway, it made her smile to think about them.

"We were part of a medical convoy heading to New Orleans," Montez said as they trudged through dangling fronds and towering oaks. Magdalys had been dreading hearing this story, and she'd been dying to hear it. She just hated the thought of her brother getting hurt. "Mostly stegos. A few brachys. There were, what? Thirty-five of us at the outset?"

"Forty-two," Corporal Wolfgang Hands said. "We lost seven in the raptor rider attack crossing the Mississippi that first day out."

"Dang." Tom Summers rubbed his wide, freckled face. "Been through so many shoot-outs, I blanked that one out."

"We all do it," Montez said. Magdalys looked at him, that long face that had seemed to grow so much older in the few months he'd been away. What had he had to erase from his young, tired mind? What would she?

"Anyway," Tom said, "Montez was asleep for the first half of the journey."

"Ha!" Montez ran a hand along the back of his head. "Yes, just a pleasant nap is all."

Magdalys was still soggy, and her boots made squishy noises with each step, and she was itchy and she kept swinging between being ecstatic she'd found her brother and terrified that they would all be massacred at any moment.

Which, she realized, hopping over a little stream, was exhausting. "What happened?" She didn't want to know. She needed to know. But she definitely didn't want to know.

Montez made the same shrugging motion he'd done since he was a kid and didn't have a good answer for something. Then he looked away.

Mapper slid his small hand around Magdalys's and squeezed once, then let go.

"General Banks had us stationed at Milliken's Bend to support General Grant's siege of Vicksburg," Wolfgang said. "General Banks is . . . ah . . ."

"Dull," Montez suggested.

"Duller than a rock," Tom added.

"A political general, is what I was going to say," Wolfgang insisted. "But it is said that General Banks was once having a conversation with a piece of wood, and the wood died of boredom."

Mapper sputtered on the water he'd been drinking. "Dang!"

"He's no General Grant, let's put it like that," Wolfgang said. "If someone gives him an order, he might get around to it one day."

"If there's an election coming up," Tom put in.

"Which, fortunately, there is," Wolfgang said. "Next year, in fact. So maybe something will actually happen around here for once. Anyway, they'd mostly been tasking us with nonsense labor jobs, on account of us being the Negro units and them still being on the fence about whether or not we were 'civilized' enough to be commanded to kill people."

Tom and Montez scoffed and shook their heads.

"When we weren't digging ditches and drilling combat maneuvers," Tom said, "we spent most of the time playing cards."

"And on target practice," Montez put in.

"Turned out, it wasn't up to the folks whether to throw us into combat," Wolfgang said. "Combat found us."

"The Rebs sent a raptor rider unit up from Texas to try and break the general's siege and bring relief to Vicksburg," Tom explained.

Montez smiled grimly. "But to break the siege, they had to get to the siege. And we were between them and the rest of the Union Army."

"They threw everything they had at us," Wolfgang said. "Came streaming over the flimsy defenses around our camp one morning before sunrise. It was hand-to-hand combat almost from the get-go."

The three men looked at each other, then back at Magdalys and Mapper.

Hand-to-hand combat. That meant none of that shooting

from far away and wondering whether you'd hit anyone. No sending dinos off to do the nasty work. You had to look your enemy right in the face and either take their life or let them take yours. She shuddered. No wonder Montez had been so ready to get that head shot on Drek.

"And one thing about being a black soldier in this fight," Wolfgang said. "There ain't no prisoner of war, being treated humanely, no treaty, no exchanges like it is with the white soldiers. Cuz we ain't human to them, see. I mean, we ain't even human to some of the ones on our own side. If the Confederates catch you, they'll probably kill you straightaway, right then and there."

"That's why," Tom said, "when your brother took a rifle butt to the back of the head, I threw him over my shoulder and pulled back toward the river."

Magdalys looked at Montez. His face was blank; he just trudged on beside her, looking straight ahead.

"He'd already saved my life a couple times, so we ain't really even, not yet," Tom said.

"Did not," Montez muttered. "Just made sure you had the medicine you needed when you caught that fever, that's all."

Wolfgang made a grunting noise. "Had to steal it from the medical tent since they wouldn't give it to us, so that is saving his life, son." He looked at Magdalys. "More of us die from disease than anything else out here. There's a whole lot of ways of being a hero. Especially these days."

"Anyway," Tom went on, "when I made it to the river, the

armored aquatic units were rolling up. Man, I never seen anything like it. Sauropods all covered in metal plates from neck to tail, and cannons mounted on either flank letting loose, mortar after mortar crashing up into the air like thunder from below."

"If it wasn't for them and those boys in the Louisiana Native Guard, we'da been toast," Wolfgang said.

"We met them!" Mapper yelled. "They were at Chickamauga!"

Montez's eyes were wide. "You've had quite an adventure, huh, sis?"

"Alright, everyone, hold march," Wolfgang said, stopping and glancing out at the darkening forest around them. Everyone else stopped too. They stood in a small clearing amidst a grove of pine and cypress trees. "Save it for a bedtime story. We bivouac here."

CHAPTER SIX
MEET THE 9TH

"**H**EY, MAGS," PRIVATE Briggs said while she and
Mapper tried and failed to set up the military-issued tent
the others had given them.

"What's up? No, Mapper! That peg goes over here!"

"That's where I put it last time, and the whole thing fell apart."

"That's cuz you put it in upside down!"

"Did not!"

"Hey, Mags," Briggs said again. "And Map Kid."

"Map*er*," Mapper said.

"Yeah?" Magdalys said.

"You know why Toussaint and I were in the front when we
were marching earlier?"

"Oh, here we go," Toussaint groaned from inside the tent
he and Briggs had already set up.

Magdalys stopped what she was doing and cocked her head at the tall, stocky soldier. "Uh . . . to make sure —"

"Reeee —" Briggs started to announce.

"RECONNAISSANCE!!" the others all yelled at once.

"That's right!" Briggs said. "That's why they call me Reconnaissance Briggs."

Magdalys and Mapper blinked at him. "Okay," she said.

"No one calls him that," Toussaint said, crawling out of the tent and shaking his head. "Literally no one has ever called you that, man." He looked at Magdalys and Mapper, who had both shrugged and gone back to messing with the tent. "He been trying to get himself a nickname since he mustered in. Pay no mind. And anyway, that wasn't reconnaissance."

"Was too!" Briggs insisted.

"Not really. We were just the front guard. We weren't scouting out enemy positions or nothin'."

"But we would've been if we'da stumbled on 'em."

"Feel like if it's gonna be part of your nickname," Mapper pointed out, "you oughta know what it is pretty well."

"He does," Corporal Hands assured them, walking up with a steamy tin cup of coffee. "He just really wants whatever it is we're doing to be that, so he tries to make it work. All he's ever wanted to do is be a spy, but when he tried to join the intelligence divisions, they said they weren't taking Negroes so . . . here we are."

"Reconnaissance," Briggs muttered, taking the tent pegs from Magdalys and plugging them into the soft dirt.

"Oh, uh, thanks," she said. Toussaint helped Mapper spread the tarp out and get it in position.

"Now, Razorclaw Jones," Private Bijoux said, walking up next to Wolfgang. He was tall and lanky, probably about seventeen, and had a jagged scar running down the center of his face. "That's a nickn — a nickn — a nickn-ni-ni-ni . . ."

His wide eyes linked with Magdalys's. *A nickname*, she almost said but didn't. Bijoux looked scared, like a train was zooming toward him. He closed his eyes, shook his head.

Wolfgang signaled her and Mapper to wait. Briggs and Toussaint just kept working away on the tent.

"A nickn — a nickn — a nickn —" Bijoux said, then: "A nickname!"

"I mean, the boy can shoot," Wolfgang acknowledged without missing a beat.

Magdalys still wasn't used to the idea that her brother was a crack-shot sniper. Still . . . there were worse things to be known for. And she was proud of him, she had to admit.

"F-fire's li-li-li-li-lit," Bijoux reported. Then he nodded at Magdalys and Mapper, saluted Wolfgang, and headed off.

"He was on the front when the raptor raiders breached our lines," Wolfgang said, saving Magdalys the trouble of asking. "Got jumped by one right as they came through. Pinned and slashed right across the face." He frowned. "It's a miracle he didn't go blind, to be honest."

"Miracle he survived at all," Toussaint said. "I was there."

"Wow," Mapper said.

"The beast nearly took his head off." Toussaint tapped the saber scabbard hanging from his belt. Grinned. "Then I took its head off."

Even with all she'd been through, Magdalys couldn't imagine the level of combat these men had survived. How could Bijoux face dinos again, let alone ride them into battle, after what had happened? Still — he hadn't seemed to be afraid of the dactyls or the toads. "And that's when he started . . . ?" She wasn't sure what to say. It seemed rude somehow, to talk about it.

"To stutter? No," Toussaint said. "The stuttering is normal for him. After the attack, he stopped talking completely. I don't think he said another word until — till we got to the mansion, right, Corp?"

Wolfgang nodded. "That's right."

"He actually used to stutter when we were kids back in the Lower 9th. Everyone in the neighborhood kinda helped him out and he got past it, but it comes back now and then. Guess the raptor attack knocked out his speech entirely for a while though."

"Best thing to do is just let him finish his sentence," Wolfgang said. "Don't try to do it for him."

"Gotya," Mapper and Magdalys said at the same time.

That crisp smoky scent wafted through the air. The last time Magdalys had been around a campfire, it was amidst a huge division of the Army of the Cumberland, hundreds and hundreds of Union soldiers, and sure, they hadn't all seemed too friendly, but at least they were more or less on her side.

Now the forest had grown very dark around them; they were about as deep into enemy territory as you could get; and a whole army of Confederates was camped out between them and the only safe haven around. She glanced over at Mapper and could tell from his gloomy expression that he was probably thinking pretty much the same thing. She put a hand on his shoulder.

"C'mon, y'all," Wolfgang Hands said. "These kids owe us some stories."

CHAPTER SEVEN
CAMPFIRE, NO SHENANIGANS

THE SMALL FIRE crackled and popped as Magdalys told the tale — how she'd been at the Zanzibar Savannah Theater with Mapper, Two Step, Amaya, and Sabeen to see Halsey and Cymbeline Crunk perform *The Tempest* when the Draft Riots broke out in Manhattan, and when they'd finally made it back to the Colored Orphan Asylum, they found it burned to the ground and old Mr. Calloway murdered by the rioters.

"No," Montez gasped. He put his face in his hands and let out a low sob.

Magdalys got up and sat next to him, one arm draped over his shoulders. In a weird way, she was relieved. He'd gotten so stony when they were talking about how he'd been injured, she'd wondered if he had started blocking off all emotions just to cope. It was hard to see him so sad, but at least he could still feel something.

"He worked at the orphanage . . . always looked out for us," Montez told the others. "His son is with the Massachusetts 54th. I wonder if he knows." He shook his head. "All this death we seen but . . . this hurts."

Magdalys just nodded, rubbing his back. She still felt that wretched recoil in the pit of her stomach when she thought about it, and the old man's face still came to her sometimes when she was trying to go to sleep. "I know. I'm sorry."

"It's something different when it's folks back home," Bijoux said. "My pops died a —" He paused, mouth open as if gasping for air, and Magdalys wasn't sure if it was his stutter or that he was overcome with emotion. "— few months ago, just up and died and . . . I was over here, trying to stay alive. I still got my moms and sis but . . . nothing's felt the same since."

Montez shook his head. "I didn't know, man . . ."

"Sorry for your loss, Roca," Wolfgang said. "And you, Bijoux." The other soldiers muttered their condolences.

"Go on," Montez said, wiping his eyes. "What happened next?"

Mapper told the next part of the saga, with occasional tidbits from Magdalys: escaping to Brooklyn with the Crunks; finding a home on Dactyl Hill, even if it was just for a few days; hanging out at the Bochinche with David Ballantine and Louis Napoleon and Miss Bernice; and meeting Redd, the cutlass-wielding pirate who helped the Vigilance Committee sometimes and went with them on a mission out into New York Harbor to stop Magistrate Richard Riker and his Kidnapping Club from sending the other orphans off to slavery.

The soldiers listened in awe as Magdalys told them about finding Stella the giant pteranodon, who got them out of more than a few jams, including an epic shoot-out at the Dactyl Hill Penitentiary, and how they'd all flown south to find Montez and fallen in with General Sheridan's division of the Army of the Cumberland, where they'd met Hannibal and the Native Guard and gotten caught up in the Battle of Chickamauga along the way, and then finally made it to New Orleans but had to leave Two Step and Sabeen trapped in Chattanooga and how Amaya had run off to find her dad.

Montez blinked at his sister. "Wow."

"There's something else though," Wolfgang said, searching her with his eyes. "Your mission."

She nodded. "General Grant, he . . ." None of it felt real, somehow. The conversation at the Saint Charles Hotel had been just that morning at dawn, but it seemed like years ago. She pulled the general's letter out of her jacket pocket; already it was wrinkled and soggy from everything she'd been through. She handed it to the corporal.

"Well, I'll be," Wolfgang said, squinting at it in the firelight. "The US Army has given your sister here the authority to create her own special dinowarriors unit."

"What?" Montez and Tom said at the same time.

"Tasked," Wolfgang read, "with rooting out and apprehending the agents of the covert organization known as the Knights of the Golden Circle, in particular their dinomasters and the upper ranks of their leadership."

"How?" Montez gasped.

Wolfgang lowered the letter, stared at Magdalys. "How indeed?"

As she always did in these moments, Magdalys thought about her friend Redd. Besides being a swashbuckler and freedom fighter, he was neck and neck with Cymbeline for being the coolest person Magdalys had ever met. *I wasn't born in a body most people would call a boy's*, he'd told her right before they'd stormed the penitentiary back in Dactyl Hill. *I had to, you know, learn not to let what other folks thought of me determine how I thought about myself.* He had put that huge grin of his away when he said it, and Magdalys had tried to imagine how hard it must've been growing up being called the wrong gender all the time. The matrons back at the Colored Orphan Asylum used to insist on calling her Margaret, which made Magdalys bristle, but that didn't even compare, not really. Redd told her she couldn't mumble about her magic: *That ain't how power works.* And since then, she'd done her best to own what she had, what she was.

But it was still hard. Even though now she'd met at least three other people who could connect to dinos with their minds (two of them Confederates, unfortunately) and had already announced to this new squad that she was the best dinowrangler in the world, it was still hard to actually say what her special magic was out loud.

"Here's how," she said, and closed her eyes, reached out with her mind like she always did. She had figured she'd stretch her thoughts toward the forest — there were sure to be some lizards crawling around nearby. Instead, a quiet muttering caught her attention much closer to where she sat. Right on the other side of the fire, in fact.

"M-Milo!" Bijoux yelped as his jacket pocket began to wriggle.

"Milo?" Wolfgang said, raising an eyebrow. "Who in the —"

Breeka breeka breeka, the muttering resolved into. A tiny lizard head poked its way out of Bijoux's collar, then it yawned, revealing razor-sharp teeth.

On either side of Bijoux, Toussaint and Briggs leapt up and took a step away. "It's a raptor, man!" Briggs yelled.

Breeka breeka breeka! Milo chortled on within Magdalys. It wasn't just a tiny dino, she realized, it was a newly hatched.

"I know — know — know what h-h-h-*he* is," Bijoux said indignantly.

"Oh boy," Montez said.

Wolfgang shook his head. "How did you — Where did you?"

Milo crawled all the way out of the jacket and slid smoothly into the crook of Bijoux's elbow. He had a long tail and tiny little front claws, and Magdalys could already tell those powerful hind legs were going to be a force to be reckoned with.

The raptor stretched, then curled up, muttered *breeka* once, and went back to sleep.

"It was that f-first night at the m-m-mansion," Bijoux explained. He looked at Magdalys and Mapper. "I was in the attic room. T-top floor. I heard a, like a, a scratching noise. Just barely. It was so quiet. Looked under the b-b-b-bed and that's where I found them."

"*Them?*" Toussaint demanded. "You got more of 'em?"

Bijoux shook his head. "Annnnnnnn . . ." He paused, took a breath, looking vexed with himself. "Nnnnnnnneot."

"Whoa," Mapper said.

Magdalys had read in Dr. Barlow Sloan's Dinoguide that raptors would sometimes keep their eggs safe by making their nests high up in the branches of live oaks. A deserted mansion would probably be like the best kind of protection, she figured.

"At f-f-first I was sssssss-s-scared of them," Bijoux admitted. "Even though they were just eggs. I mean, the m-m-m-m-mom could come b-back anyt-t-t-time. But then I remembered that raptors really don't like people; they're sh-sh-sh-shy."

"Didn't seem shy at Milliken's Bend," Briggs grumbled.

"They are shy," Magdalys said. She'd practically memorized the lengthy chapter Dr. Sloan had written on them. She hadn't ridden one yet, but they both fascinated and frightened her. And Redd's busted old raptor, Reba, was one of Magdalys's favorite dinos. "That's why they make such fierce fighting mounts. They hate people, so they feel threatened when you ride 'em into a crowd, and that's why they lash out. Nothing more dangerous than a threatened dino."

"Especially one with twelve-inch toenails," Briggs said. Then he smacked his face. "Aw, man. Sorry, Bijoux."

Bijoux waved him off. "A-a-anyway, it was cold that night, so I covered them with a bl-bl-blanket. And the next day, ju-ju-ju-ju-just Milo hatched. The rest, the rest st-st-st-stopped scra-scra-scra-scra-scratching."

"You fed that thing, didn't you?" Toussaint demanded.

"I —"

"We were barely making it on hardtack crumbs and the rotten scraps we could salvage from that mansion's pantries, and you were giving food to the same monster that —"

"I f-f-f-ed him half of my p-p-p-portion!" Bijoux said. "That's all! Didn't t-take away from anyone else."

"So you would've starved yourself so it could live?"

"It's what got him talking again," Magdalys said quietly. Everyone looked at her. She didn't know how she knew it, but it was a fact that seemed to just sit there, looking at her. And Toussaint had said Bijoux hadn't said a word since the attack until they got to the mansion.

"It's true," Bijoux said. "I d-d-don't understand it, but it's true." He held the tiny raptor close and it nuzzled him, still sleeping. "I'm s-s-s-sorry!"

"Don't be," Briggs said. "You didn't take none of my food. What do I care? I'm just glad you're talking again."

Bijoux smiled at him.

"I'm going to sleep," Toussaint said. "Y'all can keep feeding your little pets while we go hungry, but I, for one, plan to get out of this mess alive. Whatever it takes." He got up, shot a cold glance at Bijoux, and headed off to the tents.

"Alright, alright," Wolfgang said. "We all need some shut-eye. Got a long day tomorrow. I'll explain on the way. And, Private Roca?"

"Sir, yes sir!" Magdalys and Montez both said.

Wolfgang sighed. "This is gonna take some getting used to, huh? Private Girl Roca."

"Sir, yes sir!"

He handed her General Grant's letter. "That won't do either. Anyway, you've still got some explaining to do. We'll talk in the morning."

CHAPTER EIGHT
WHAT LIES AHEAD

"**YOU KNOW,**" **MAPPER** said as they trudged along through the swampy wilderness at dawn the next morning, "we're actually going directly toward the enemy encampment."

"Girl Private Roca!" Corporal Hands hollered.

Magdalys jogged a few steps forward so she was beside Wolfgang and Mapper. "Sir, yes sir!"

"No, that's not it either. We'll figure it out. When did you acquire the friendship of this peculiar little genius?"

"Sir, you mean Private Mapper, sir? Er . . . Private Kyle? Ah . . ."

"Mapper will do fine," Wolfgang said. "We in the Louisiana 9th believe in nicknames, as you may have noticed."

"RECONNAISSANCE!" a voice yelled from up ahead.

"Not you, Briggs!" Wolfgang growled. "How does one expect to be good at reconnaissance when one can't keep one's mouth shut?"

"One heard that," Briggs called.

"Good!" Wolfgang retorted. "That's why I said it. Anyway." He glanced at Magdalys. "Yes, Mapper."

"We've known each other for . . ." She thought back. Mapper had been around for as long as she could remember, and he'd been plotting mischief and studying atlases in the library since before he knew how to read. "Forever."

"And how exactly do you deal with him being a know-it-all?" Wolfgang asked.

"Aw, man," Mapper said.

Magdalys rolled her eyes. "You just get used to it, I guess. Thing is, it's easier to put up with a know-it-all when he really does know it all. Plus, I'm positive I never would've made it here if it wasn't for him."

Mapper raised one shoulder and then the other like he didn't know what to do with himself. "Geez, Mags . . ."

"He's one of my best friends," she finished.

Wolfgang nodded approvingly. "Very good, then. In fact, Mapper, you are correct: We are headed directly back toward the enemy encampment." He glanced around. "Louisiana 9th, squad up! I want you all to hear this."

Montez and Tom double-timed it from behind them, and up ahead, Bijoux, Briggs, and Toussaint slowed down. Magdalys noticed Toussaint hadn't said a word to Bijoux since the night before; in fact, he'd barely said a word at all. But Milo the raptor was perched happily on Bijoux's shoulder, blinking at the bright forest around them without a care in the world.

They all kept marching, but slower now, in a tight formation around Wolfgang.

"The enemy is dead ahead," he said. "And beyond them lies our beloved city, the only place most of us call home. And home matters more than just about anything else in this world besides your name, the ones you love, and your honor. Ya hear?"

"Sir, yes sir!" Magdalys, Mapper, and the Louisiana 9th said as one.

"Good. But keep it down a little. We're getting a little too close to be that loud."

"Sir, yes sir!" they all whispered.

"Now, we've been through some things, all of us." His eyes met with each of the soldiers' in his squad, then Mapper's and Magdalys's. "And I know all we want to do is get home and wash up and sleep in a real bed without these racists shooting at us everywhere we go."

"Amen, amen," Briggs said.

"But the fact is, we may not have a home to come back to if what appears to be going down is really what's going down."

"You think they getting ready to move on New Orleans?" Bijoux asked, amidst mutters and groans.

"They better not," Toussaint said. "They'll get the whupping of their lives if they try."

"That is what I think," Wolfgang said. "We've never seen

a troop amassment in Louisiana of that size. Not since the Union took New Orleans, anyway. But with Vicksburg fallen and whatever defeat our boys just suffered in Tennessee, well, there's probably some freed-up brigands roaming around now, the way I figure it, and we know the state militia has been begging Richmond for troops for a while now. Looks like they finally got 'em. And I wouldn't be so sure they won't be able to, Private Toussaint. They nearly recaptured Baton Rouge a few months back, and if it wasn't for our sauropod fleet, they would've."

"He has a point," Briggs said.

"And last I heard," Wolfgang went on, "Banks had orders to send most of the soldiers they do have out of New Orleans."

"That's right!" Magdalys said suddenly, remembering her conversation in the Saint Charles Hotel. "General Grant told me that Emperor Maximilian is massing troops at a town called Matamoros on the Mexican border, so General Banks has to deal with that with whatever units he has left. That's why he couldn't spare any to send on the rescue mission to get you guys."

Some grumbling rose up as the soldiers exchanged irritated glances.

"They was really about to let us die for some foreign-policy mess," Toussaint mumbled. "Problems in a whole other country more important than their own soldiers."

"You surprised?" Briggs scoffed. "We nothin' to them." He

swatted the air, disgust on his face. "Ditchdiggers and cannon fodder."

"It ain't that," Wolfgang said. "But I hear where y'all coming from."

"What is it, then?" Toussaint demanded.

"The French put Emperor Maximilian in place, toppled President Juárez's government to do it. Juárez's men been fighting back, but they all in retreat now, from what I hear. Hiding in the mountains and launching guerrilla attacks. Point is, the French been flirting with the idea of supporting the Confederacy for a while now. If they get a foothold in Mexico, that'll open up a whole trade route of arms and supplies to the enemy, see? And then they'll attack from the south and we'll be caught between two massive armies: the Franco-Mexican Imperialists and the newly reinvigorated Confederates. The Union will fall and the dream of those Knights of the Golden Circle that Magdalys told us about will come true: a slavery empire reaching across the Americas."

Everyone got quiet for a moment, and the click and buzz of the swamp rose around them. Grant had said something to that effect, Magdalys remembered now, but she'd been so caught up in her anger — the very army that Montez had risked his life for was abandoning him! — that she hadn't really wrapped her mind around what that meant.

But the corporal was right: With the Imperial Army massing at the Mexican border, the Golden Circle was on the brink of going from a conspiracy whispered in back channels, a shadow, to something very real. And with the Knights' dino-masters in the fight, they'd be nearly unstoppable.

"What that means," Wolfgang said, breaking everyone out of their worried reveries, "is that New Orleans really is about to fall. They've surely gotten word about the plans to send troops to the border — the Confederates have eyes and ears in every gin joint and back alley of that city. It's probably part of their plan: get the troops sent off to deal with the French and then amass troops and invade while no one's there to defend New Orleans."

"Which means . . ." Montez said.

"We have some important work to do," Wolfgang said.

Everyone looked at Briggs, who was staring off into space.

"*Very* important work," Wolfgang said.

"What kind of work?" Montez asked pointedly.

"Work that involves scoping out enemy positions and reporting back, perhaps?" Tom suggested.

Briggs blinked but didn't seem to be listening.

Wolfgang threw his hands up. "Oh my goodness! I give up! Briggs!"

Briggs snapped a salute. "Sir, yes sir!"

"As long as we've known you, you haven't shut up about —"

"RECONNAISSANCE!!"

"And now, *finally*! We come to a moment when —"

Briggs widened his eyes and glanced around. "RECONNAISSANCE? Sir?"

Wolfgang sighed. "Yes, Briggs. Reconnaissance."

"RECONNAISSANCE BRIGGS, REPORTING FOR DUTY!"

Toussaint rubbed his eyes. "Can we leave him behind?"

"Unfortunately, no," Wolfgang said. "We're gonna need all hands on deck for this one. Especially" — he turned his glare directly on Magdalys — "this young lady."

CHAPTER NINE
RECONNAISSANCE!!

Part 1: A Distraction

JUST A DISTURBANCE, *not an attack*, Wolfgang had said. *But a big disturbance. Huge, even.*

Magdalys sat very still on a thick oak tree branch and scowled. It was only a day earlier, fending off the legions of dinoattacks that Drek sent her way, that she'd realized just how much deeper her powers really were; she still didn't know the full extent of them. She could break through his hold on a dino's mind. She could sway the paths of multiple attacking pteros at once. What else was she capable of?

"You ready?" Montez asked from the next branch over. Wolfgang had detailed him and Bijoux as her protection unit.

"What's the signal for me to start?" Magdalys had asked just before they split up.

"There is none," Wolfgang said with a chuckle. "You're the signal for us to start."

She'd grimaced. "Right." Then she dapped Mapper and waved at the others as they walked off into the thick woods.

Now the marsh seemed very, very quiet from way up in this tree. Magdalys had spent most of her time in the Atchafalaya either soaring above the canopy or down in the swampy terrain. This in-between place was a whole new and peaceful side of it. Too peaceful. They were on a recon mission, after all, and the world around them being quiet meant that they had to be extra, extra quiet if they didn't want to get caught and blow the whole thing.

She looked at Montez and nodded. He raised his rifle and clicked the scope into place. "Thanks for saving us, by the way."

She rolled her eyes. "You've already thanked me like a million times, big bro. It's cool."

"Yeah, but I didn't know the whole thing about the army giving us up for dead so they could concentrate on Mexico. It just . . . it's another level to it, you know? You came to get us anyway, just you and Mapper."

She wobbled her head, not sure what to do with his words.

"Hey, Private R-R-R-Roca," Bijoux said from the branch on her other side. They both looked over to find him snickering. "Ah, never g-g-g-gets old. I meant the gi — the gi — the gi — the g-girl one though."

"It got old the first time it happened," Montez grumbled.

"What's up, Bijoux?" Magdalys asked.

"I had a — a — a favor to ask." He clicked his own rifle scope into position and started loading bullets into the opened barrel. With a shuffle and squeak, Milo shoved his little snout out from Bijoux's collar and glanced around.

"Don't send Milo into the fray?" Magdalys asked. "I would never." She winked at him. "He's part of the Louisiana 9th now. That's a United States service member. Can't just have him rolling around like some common swamp dino."

The smile that broke out across Bijoux's face was bigger than any she'd seen on him. "Good lookin', lil' sis."

"Hey, hey," Montez called. "She's got one big brother in this squad and he's me, buddy."

"Alright, guys, quiet down," Magdalys warned. "I'd rather get this done without you both having to pick off attacking Confederates while I'm trying to concentrate, thank you very much."

"Yeah, yeah, yeah," Montez mumbled.

She closed her eyes. Let the click and clack of more bullets being loaded fade away amidst the other chirps and buzzes of the underbrush. Tuned into the wider, deeper rumble of the living universe around her. Quieted her fast-beating heart. Searched.

Dizz's quiet, bubbly *fubba fubba* came first. He stood at the ready on a branch a few feet above them. Then the gentle *breeka*s of little Milo, nuzzled in Bijoux's coat pocket.

She left them and sent her wandering thoughts out farther into the dank underbrush around them.

There. It didn't take long. She'd figured it wouldn't be hard to find dinos in such a dense and wild forest, but you never knew. . . . War had a way of toppling the natural order of things.

Pateeeeeeee patee pateeeeeee, crooned a nearby duckbill. She didn't know how she knew what it was, but the image appeared so suddenly and clearly in her mind, it had to be. Another responded from not far away: *Pateeeeeee pateeeeeee.*

What else? A twittering, snarling family of sinorniths — wild ones, not the Bog Marauder mounts — was perched in a tree not far away. And a whole crew of microdactyls fluttered overhead.

That should do it.

The Confederate camp was a little ways north of them and a little to the east, according to Mapper. She tried to imagine it from the glimpse she'd seen yesterday: rows and rows of gray-clad soldiers standing in formation amidst shabby tents. A few divisions of ironclad artillery stegos stomping impatiently in the dust. One command brachy, its long neck reaching up over the treetops. And spinebacks, those long snouts and sharp teeth gnashing.

Drek was in there somewhere, plotting and conspiring. She'd have to find him, somehow.

But she also couldn't get distracted. There was one task before her now, and it would take all her focus.

Taking a deep breath, she sent her thoughts back out to the

dinos around her: three, no, four duckbills, twelve sinorniths, and, hardest of all, about three dozen microdactyls.

She'd do them one group at a time, she decided, rather than try to send them all at once. That way they'd crash through in waves and add to the confusion. That's what she hoped anyway. Plus, she wasn't sure if she could manage them all at once. Not yet . . .

With an exhale, she snapped the duckbills to attention and felt their curiosity turn to a strange kind of . . . was that respect? as her mind clicked with theirs. *I need your help*, she thought toward them. They probably didn't understand English — she knew that — but the meaning of her words would carry over.

With a little swivel of her head, she indicated where they were to go, her thoughts wandering northward through the trees.

Run! Magdalys thought. *Trample! Charge!*

An eruption of stomps and hoots and rustling trees off to her left let her know the message had been received.

Magdalys smiled and opened her eyes to shoot Montez a knowing glance.

He just blinked and shook his head. "Amazing."

Eyes closed. Another reach through the forest. The sudden run of the duckbills had spooked the sinorniths some — they had fluttered up to the top level of the canopy and were flapping their wings and cawing, getting ready to soar off to a less dicey part of the forest.

No you don't, Magdalys thought, feeling them fall within her mind's grasp one by one. *How 'bout this way instead . . .*

All seven leapt into the sky at the same time. She glanced up as their dark brown bodies glided past overhead, wings spread.

"Beautiful," Magdalys whispered. "Now for the —"

Gunshots rang out up ahead, then the low rumble of mortar fire.

"Hooboy," Bijoux said, raising his rifle.

She looked back and forth between him and her brother. "What does it mean? What do we do?"

"You have more dinos to send?" Montez asked.

She nodded. "Pteros actually. But —"

"Stick to the plan," he said, aiming at the forest below.

"St-stick to the p-plan," Bijoux confirmed, swinging his rifle up toward the sky.

Magdalys nodded, tried not to think about Mapper, and Wolfgang, and Tom, and —

She closed her eyes. *C'mon, little guys*, Magdalys urged, her thoughts blipping between the fussy coos and squawks of the microdactyl swarm. *C'mon, c'mon, c'mon.*

More gunfire kept blasting out in sudden staccato bursts, and every few minutes another artillery shell would whistle and bang up ahead. But she couldn't get distracted. Couldn't get caught up thinking about what might be happening to Mapper, or —

Fubbafubbafubbafubbafubbba, the microdactyls sang in little high-pitched imitations of their larger ptero cousins.

"Gotya!" Magdalys whispered, her mind clicking into that sharp synchronicity with theirs. *Now go!* she commanded. There was no time to request. No time for politeness. The swarm flitted out across the sky, suddenly silent and determined. They felt her urgency and moved with it along their wings.

The first duckbills had probably reached the camp and caused some mild uproar, and the boys had taken it as their cue, Magdalys figured. They must've hurtled up into the sky on Grappler and Beans to get a good view of the camp. And Confederates probably spotted them, and . . . "Let's go," Magdalys said, standing on the branch and making her way back toward the trunk.

Already, Dizz was flapping his wings, now hopping down toward them.

"Ready," Montez said, his rifle strapped snugly to his backpack. "Bijoux, we'll meet you at the toads."

"Stay safe," Bijoux said, climbing down the tree. Milo blinked up at them from his shoulder. Then hopped onto the tree and scrambled up. "Milo!"

Magdalys yelped as the tiny raptor leapt onto her leg, his little claws piercing through her pants into her skin. "Hey!"

Milo made his way right to her satchel and crawled in, tail disappearing last.

Magdalys looked down at Bijoux. "I didn't . . ." she said, shaking her head. "I swear I didn't tell him to do that!"

Bijoux blinked, then nodded. "It's oh — it's oh — it's oh — it's okay, M-Magdalys, I pr-pr-pr-promise."

"But —"

"He goes wh-wh-wh-where he's needed m-m-m-most. If he's with you, it m-m-m-means, maybe I don't need him as much." He smiled shakily. "F-for now, anyway."

She was about to offer to bring Milo to him, but Bijoux just shrugged and made his way down the tree.

CHAPTER TEN
RECONNAISSANCE!!

Part 2: Dactyl's-Eye View

"**U**P!" **MAGDALYS SAID,** the wind already whipping across her face as the swampy forest became a blur below. "Heeyah!" Dizz spun a slow circle as he climbed, showing them the miles and miles of Atchafalaya around them, the billowing clouds against the pale blue sky. Somewhere out there, way, way in the distance, was New Orleans — the city was a little bit of safety in a murderous world, but it wouldn't be for long, the way things were going.

Behind her, Montez was holding on for dear life. "Are you sure this isn't too hi —"

"Hold tight," Magdalys said, and urged Dizz higher. He

was the fastest ptero she'd ever ridden (although Grappler was the best at fighting). Dizz loved turning barrel rolls, which freaked out most riders. But who cared about barrel rolls when you were facing directly up and the only thing around you was sky, pure sky?

The best way to get a look at an enemy encampment was to get as high above it as you could. That's what Wolfgang had said, and it made perfect sense. Plus, the sinornith patrols probably couldn't even make it this high. She leveled Dizz out and swooped down a little to get beneath a passing cloud.

The shooting and shelling had stopped, but Magdalys wasn't sure whether that was a good thing or ominous. She scanned the forest below, caught sight of their winged shadow gliding over the treetops.

"There!" Montez said. "The camp."

She followed his point to an open field that looked like it had become a living thing — dinos and soldiers swarmed across it amidst tents and supply wagons. "Guess the distraction worked. Do you see the others?"

Something flickered over the trees near the camp: a sinornith rider, Magdalys realized. There was another. Where were they headed? "See what's happening down there," Magdalys yelled to her brother over the whipping wind. She swooped lower.

Montez lifted his rifle and, blinking against the rush of air, peered through the sight. "Keep her steady."

"Him," Magdalys said. "Don't roll your eyes at me!"

"I see one of 'em. Mapper, I think. North, northwest of the camp."

"Um . . ."

Montez shook his head and pointed. "Over there. You're gonna have to learn this stuff, sis."

"I just mustered in yesterday! Give me a break." She narrowed her eyes, taking Dizz into a long downward swoop. *Bad time to barrel roll,* she advised him, feeling that familiar tug to one side. *Montez would probably freak out.*

Dizz let out a curt *fubba* and grumpily stayed upright.

Something blue moved in that sea of green and brown. Mapper! And Tom was beside him, looking through a spyglass at the Confederate camp. They both sat astride Beans, who was perched amidst the branches, glancing from side to side. Nervous probably.

Sinoriding Bog Marauders swerved and dove nearby, hunting them, no doubt. Where were the others though?

"What do we do?" Magdalys asked, grateful to be with someone who would actually have an answer to that question.

"Stick to the plan," Montez said. "We have a mission. Now see what you can make out of the camp. Then we'll see what we can do about the others."

Magdalys swung into a curve, keeping them higher than the sinorniths, and tilted Dizz just enough to get a good view of the campsite below.

Total disarray. That was about all she could say about it at first glance. Soldiers scattered every which way, some pulling on their gray uniforms as they went. Her family of micro-dactyls rushed through, picking at people and snatching up whatever small objects they could get their beaks around. The duckbills stomped back and forth, wrecking tents and kicking up ash from last night's campfires. Half-dressed soldiers were trying to capture them, not having much luck. Off to the side, the sinorniths squawked and spooked a trio of artillery stegos.

"I can't make heads or tails of it," she said. "Why did the corporal have me send in those dinos when it only made a mess of things?"

"Look harder," Montez said. "It's all right there. That's why he did that. First of all as a distraction, but second of all, if he hadn't, all we'd have to look at would be row after row of tents. How many men in each tent?"

"I don't kno —"

"Exactly!" Montez said. She'd forgotten what a know-it-all he could be when he got going. "This way, they're all out and about. And we get to see how they react when they're scram-bling for battle. Invaluable information!"

She took them in another wide loop over the camp. One of those larger tents had to be an armory, she realized. Even in the chaos, men were streaming into it and coming out with muskets in hand. The command brachy stomped impatiently at the far edge of the forest, swinging her long neck back and forth and hooting at the troops below. The brass would probably be congregating in there, Magdalys figured, discussing what to do next.

But where was Grappler with Toussaint and Briggs? And where was — As if in answer to her thoughts, a flash of red caught her eye. Earl Shamus Dawson Drek came storming out of the small building mounted on the command brachy's saddle. A large bald man hurried behind him — a general, Magdalys figured, or some high-ranking brass. He yelled something about deserting them in their hour of need, when they most required his talents, and then a slew of words that the orphanage matrons would've whupped Magdalys for even thinking.

She flew lower as Drek stomped out of sight behind some trees. Magdalys craned her neck and then gasped as he came gliding out atop the crimson dactyl he'd become so famous for riding. They soared off into the woods. The officer stood there in the dispersing cloud of dust, glaring after Drek, and finally spat and hurried back to the brachy.

"We have to go after him!" Magdalys said.

"After who?" Montez had been looking off the other side, counting troops.

"Drek, Montez! He's there! And he just flew off!"

"We follow the mission," Montez said sharply. "Recon and meet back up where we left the toads. That's it."

"This *is* recon," Magdalys said. "And Drek is *my* mission." She swung the dactyl out over the trees toward where Drek had rushed off.

"You can't just go on some wild hunt every time something pops off that you're interested in," Montez said.

That stung. *And* he was wrong. "It's not —"

"This isn't about you," Montez said. Then softened. "It isn't about me either. It's about all of us, Mags. Don't you see?"

"Yes, I see," Magdalys said, bringing Dizz down onto a branch and turning herself so she could look her brother in the eye. "And I'm trying to tell you —"

"You can't be so reckless!" Montez said.

Magdalys felt her eyes go wide as blood rushed to her face. "Reckless! Me! You! You're the —"

He looked at her, suddenly calm, his shoulders rising and falling with each heavy breath. "The one who what?"

". . . You . . ." She shook her head. It wasn't fair. None of it was fair. Not what had happened to Montez, not what was happening to them now, not this whole twisted, angry world. And she knew that. She'd given up expecting things to be fair a long time ago. But still . . .

Montez's whole horrible journey seemed to flash between them in that moment. But Magdalys had had a journey too, and they'd barely had a chance to learn about what the other had been through before things had started blowing up around them again.

She pulled General Grant's letter out of her pocket. "It's never been about me," she said, fighting off tears, trying to keep from yelling. "And this piece of paper says I *can* just go on some wild hunt every time something pops off that I'm interested in." A gunshot sounded from back at the campsite. Magdalys kept her eyes steel and stuck on her brother's. "And that's exactly what I plan to do."

More shooting.

"Fine," Montez said through clenched teeth. "But we still gotta let the others know and make sure they're not in a jam."

"Fine," Magdalys said, eyes tight. "Let's do it then and do it fast. I don't plan on letting Drek get away again."

CHAPTER ELEVEN
BACK AND AWAY AGAIN

"**A**HOY!" **MAPPER SHOUTED** from the treetops where he and Tom were crouched beside Beans. Magdalys landed Dizz alongside them and the two dactyls pecked and snapped at each other's faces affectionately.

"What happened?" Montez asked. "Where the others?"

"Toussaint and Briggs," Tom said, rubbing his eyes.

"Are they okay?" Magdalys asked, heart suddenly thumping in her ears.

"What they are," Mapper said, "is AMAZING!!"

"That is *not* how we're supposed to be doing things," Tom said.

"What happened?" Magdalys demanded. Drek was getting farther and farther away with each passing second. She had no idea how she'd find him at this point, but she had to try.

"They stumbled on some unwatched trikes on the edge of camp," Tom said. "Guess in the confusion, all their dino-wranglers went to help."

"And they snatched 'em!" Mapper said. "And rode off into the woods with 'em!"

"So the Confederates gave chase, that was that first couple blasts you heard. They *hate* when we steal their stuff." Tom chuckled, then sighed. "Anyway, I don't know what that last barrage was. We were about to go check it out when you guys showed up." He tightened the straps on Beans's saddle and gave Mapper a hand climbing up.

Magdalys was impressed at how fast Mapper had fallen in with the others — they were already working together like they went way back. She pushed down gently on Dizz to let him know they were about to take off. "We're going after Drek," Magdalys said. Dizz leaned into a squat, wings flapping. "He took off on that crimson dactyl and had an officer cursing at him to come back and everything."

"Whoa!" Mapper said.

"I gotta find out where he went that was so important," Magdalys said as they took off. "See you back at the toads!"

It was a terrible plan, Magdalys realized as they soared westward over the treetops, shadow flickering beneath them.

She'd thought maybe, *maybe*, she could somehow key into the thoughts of that red dactyl Drek was riding. Maybe she could even do it without the ptero knowing, and then follow along from above until he got wherever he was going, and then she could find out what it was he'd been in such a hurry to accomplish when his own army needed those dinomastery skills most.

But of course, the swamp was full of creatures great and small, and no matter how hard she concentrated on the passing trees below, all she could glean from the smorgasbord of calls was that there were a lot of them. Far too many to be able to sort through and find the *fubba fubba* of one dactyl.

She shouldn't have let Montez convince her to go back and check in with Mapper and Tom. Those were precious minutes, gone. They'd made all the difference. And Mapper and Tom didn't need their help!

"Can't believe you pulled rank on me," Montez said. "My own sister."

"Yeah, well . . ." *You let Drek get away*, she almost said. She bit it back though. What was the point? Inside, a hundred different dinocalls surged in a dissonant symphony. It was giving her a headache.

"What's that?" Montez asked, stretching his arm past her to point at something way up ahead.

Magdalys squinted, urging Dizz into a low dash. "What's wha — whoa!" A plume of smoke rose into the sky. Could it be? "I think I've seen that smoke before," she said as they skimmed across the treetops.

"Look," Montez said, "I know you're probably mad at me. I get it."

"Montez." She swung Dizz into a wide arc — probably wouldn't be wise to just fly directly over whatever it was smoking — then felt another barrel roll coming. "Hold tight for a sec."

"Wait, whaaaaah!!" They turned upside down momentarily and then righted again. "Whewwww, man! Does he *have* to do that?"

Magdalys smiled to herself. "I think it's a nervous thing. But also he likes to mess with people, so there's that. I try to catch him before he does it, but . . . it doesn't always work."

"Anyway! I was saying, I get why you'd be mad. You came out of nowhere and saved all our lives and I'll always be grateful for that . . ."

"I sense a big *but* coming," Magdalys said. "And I'm not really in the mood to hear it, Montez."

"I know, it's just —"

"There it is!" Magdalys yelled, veering Dizz off over the trees again before they were spotted. She'd only caught a glimpse out of the corner of her eye, but it was enough to know exactly what lay below: those rickety wooden houses rising on stilts from the murky swamp water — that same Bog Marauder headquarters they'd flown over on their way in to find Montez the day before.

This *had* to be where Drek had run off to. But why come here when he'd realized the camp was being overrun by wild dinos? Magdalys tightened her face as she brought Dizz down to a landing.

She'd just have to go in and find out.

CHAPTER TWELVE
RECONNAISSANCE!!

Part 3: Sneak and Snipe

"**W**ONDER WHERE EVERYONE went," Magdalys whispered.

They'd swept in a gradually shrinking spiral around the compound, careful to keep just out of view until they realized there was no one around to see them. Then Magdalys had brought Dizz down on a long branch reaching out over the swamp waters, and they'd dismounted to get a better look.

"Some of them were at the Confederate camp," Montez said. "How many did you see when you passed over yesterday?"

Magdalys scrunched up her face. Numbers were not her

thing, and Montez knew that. Still, she'd have to learn if she was going to be any good at this. "Maybe like twelve or . . ." She tried to picture the sinoriders clustered together. It had seemed like a lot at the time, but maybe that was fear distorting her view. "Thirty-something?"

Montez sighed through a smile. "Okay, we'll work on that counting thing. It takes some practice." It wasn't unkind — this was the patient, gentle Montez who Magdalys remembered teaching the others how to read in the orphanage library, not the battle-hardened sniper she'd found out here in the swamps. Both of those Montezes were real, and she'd simply have to learn to reconcile them with each other. Along with learning how to estimate troop numbers. And whatever else this war would demand of her . . .

"That bigger building," Montez said, pointing to a ramshackle cabin at the far end of the site.

Something fluttered and shrieked through the sky above them, and Magdalys ducked, glancing up, but it was just a passing family of microdactyls. She untensed the fingers that had wrapped themselves around her carbine grip, then looked back at the building. "You think that's where Drek is?"

"Wasn't he riding a bright red ptero?"

Magdalys followed Montez's gaze along a rickety wooden stairway that led from the door to a small floating platform beside one of the support stilts. There, Drek's crimson dactyl perched so perfectly still on a railing it looked like a statue.

"Can I shoot it?" Montez asked.

"What good would that do?" Magdalys whispered.

"Then he'd come out to see what happened and I could shoot him too."

"Montez. We gotta find out what's going on, man. And if he's dead, we can't do that. Whatever the Knights are up to, it's bigger than this one man. But he might be the key to unraveling the whole thing."

"So . . ."

"So we have to take him alive. That's the only way we'll find out what's really going on."

"I guess."

"Plus, we don't know who else is in there. But I'm about to find out. Stay here and cover me."

"Wait —"

Magdalys didn't wait. She turned and climbed onto Dizz, who was already flapping his wings eagerly, and together they soared across the camp. Montez would be mad, but he'd probably just shake his head and set up that sniper rifle of his to take whatever shot he'd need to.

She slid sidewise down the saddle as Dizz approached, then gripped it with both hands and let herself hang down. "Easy, D. Easy." He swooped down just a little farther, so the tips of her boots scraped the tin rooftop, and then she let go, landing in a crouch without too much noise, and waited as Dizz swung back around toward Montez.

The smoke had been rising from a chimney on one of the smaller houses, Magdalys noticed with satisfaction. Which meant the stone stack rising from this one should be usable. She crept over to it, trying to stay as soft on her feet as possible, and then crawled in.

She'd only spent a short time sweeping chimneys in Dactyl Hill, Brooklyn, but the feeling of that cramped, soot-covered darkness surrounding her came back in dream after dream. And now here she was again, crisp smell of charred firewood fresh in her nose as she carefully made her way lower and lower.

"And what if they are?" a nasal voice demanded. Magdalys froze. "They'll never catch up to the progress we've made already."

"Your arrogance will be the death of us all, Grandmaster." That was Drek; she was sure of it.

"Watch your tone, Shamus," a woman snapped. "And don't forget who you're addressing."

If only Magdalys could see! Ever so quietly, she crawled a few more feet down.

"My point is this," Drek said, sounding like he was restraining the growl in his voice from growing even more severe. "We think we are the hunters, but we are being hunted. That girl can't be the only one they've gathered to destroy us. Let me find her and take her out of the equation and then —"

"You are so terrified of a child!" the woman sneered. "And a Negro one at that. Pathetic."

Magdalys was caught somewhere between rage and terror. Whatever happened after this, she had a target on her back now. That much was clear. And it wouldn't go away until Drek and all the Knights of the Golden Circle were behind bars.

"She rode into battle on some kind of primordial toad, Grandmaster. And she broke my hold over the dinos I sent to destroy her. I've never seen anything like it."

Magdalys allowed herself a small flush of pride within her nervousness. Of course, her being that powerful was exactly what had now landed her in Drek's crosshairs.

"Get ahold of yourself, man," snarled the Grandmaster. "You're a class-A dinomaster with the Knights of the Golden Circle. Listen to yourself."

"My man in the Army of the Tennessee says Hewpat has been captured," Drek said.

"I've heard. Bad luck," mused the Grandmaster. "But he was our weakest member, let's be honest. And anyway, he's been rendered insensible, from what I understand, so he won't be giving up any valuable information on us anytime soon."

"And Miss Crawbell sent a gram saying she faced off with a Negro girl on a pteranodon over Chickamauga and was nearly bested."

"Elizabeth?" the woman scoffed. "Not possible."

"She wrote the gram herself, Mistress Shallows."

"It doesn't matter," the Grandmaster hissed. "What matters is the mission. That's *all* that matters. You have your orders. Here's the data you requested from our scientists. Forget the Negress. Forget everything else except the mission. Don't you see, Dinomaster Drek? This is how we win. Not at

Chattanooga. Not even in Virginia, where Lincoln has concentrated the majority of his efforts. Those pompous fools are all looking the wrong direction! And when they realize their mistake, it'll be too late! They'll be trapped in our jaws and stamped out forever."

Magdalys heard papers being shuffled. That was the key to everything, whatever it was. And there was no way they'd say their mission out loud, not when it was written down and spelled out clearly in the papers that had just been handed over. She had to get her hands on that document! But *how?*

She lowered herself to just above the edge of the fireplace.

"If someone is able to best our highest-ranked dinomaster," Drek said icily, "I think that matters a whole lot, actually."

"Not your concern," the Grandmaster said. "We'll handle the girl. You do what you're told, Drek. Now, you're to leave immediately. Is that clear? We have friendly agents among the riverboaters in New Orleans. Travel down the Mississippi and then cross the Gulf of Mexico and embed yourself with the guerrillas. I'll send two of our Sky Raiders to rendezvous with you at the site. Those documents will tell you everything else you need to know."

"What is that?!" Mistress Shallows shrieked over the metallic click of guns being cocked and chairs screeching against the floor.

"Where?" someone yelled with a booming voice Magdalys hadn't heard yet.

"Over in the shadows there!"

What was happening?

"Just a silly raptor," Drek said. "Calm down. I'll just . . ."

Magdalys heard the skittering of claws — Milo! It had to be! She'd clean forgotten that he had crawled into her satchel. And with a quick pat, she confirmed that he was indeed no longer in there. But what was he up to?

Mistress Shallows yelled: "Careful, Shamus! It's . . . Do something!"

Milo hissed and cawed and something large turned over, a table probably, and then a few shots sang out, their echoes reverberating through the stone building. Magdalys pulled out her carbine and took advantage of the ruckus to load and cock it. More yelling and skittering amidst boot stomps and the sound of paper fluttering every which way.

Why wasn't Drek able to control him?

Didn't matter. She couldn't let them hurt Milo. Bijoux would be devastated, and he'd probably never forgive her.

"Stop shooting!" the Grandmaster yelled. "Drek! What's the matter with you? Stop that dino!"

Magdalys took a deep breath and dropped into the fireplace.

CHAPTER THIRTEEN
RENDEZVOUS AND RUN

MAGDALYS LANDED RUNNING and let off two shots into the air as she burst through the room.

Maximum confusion. That was the only thing that would get her out of this alive. She kicked over a chair, swung another over a table, and elbowed past someone in a white robe standing nearby.

Guns exploded around her, but she didn't know if they were aiming for her or Milo. "That's her!" Drek yelled. She fired again, the noise deafening in that enclosed space, and then dove behind a cabinet and glanced around the other side.

There were almost a half-dozen figures in the room — way more than she'd thought — and all of them wore those long white robes, except for Drek, who sprinted toward her, still in his gray Confederate uniform.

Milo was nowhere to be seen.

"Get that dino!" someone yelled.

"Get the girl!" Drek insisted.

Magdalys aimed for his kneecap, but the shot thwunked through the wooden floor planks instead. Still, it had been enough to send Drek ducking out of the way, and that was all the time Magdalys needed to dash for the far door.

She burst into the sunlight as more shooting rang out behind her and didn't stop or glance back, just barreled full tilt across the wooden catwalk until she saw Dizz's shadow sweeping past her.

Right on time! she thought, slowing down to climb onto the railing so she could jump to where the dactyl flapped in a loop-de-looping dive.

Behind her, Drek wailed, "NOOOO!!" with so much anguish and horror that it made Magdalys stop midclimb and glance back. "Sweet Virginia!" Drek wasn't looking at her; his eyes were glued to a large, shining shape floating lifelessly in the murky water below amidst a growing circle of red. The crimson dactyl.

Drek turned, looked directly at Magdalys. "What have you done?!"

She shook her head, already reaching for Dizz.

"You killed her!" Drek suddenly had a pistol in each hand. Magdalys hadn't even seen him draw them. His whole face turned as red as his beard, and he let off shot after shot with each gun.

"Go!" Magdalys yelled, grabbing tight to Dizz's stirrups as bullets whizzed past. There wasn't time to climb all the way up. "GO!"

"I'll kill you!" Drek raged below her. "You're dead, girl!"

"What did you do?" Magdalys demanded, sliding down from Dizz's saddle onto the branch that Montez was still stretched out along, squinting through his rifle sight.

"Canceled any plans Drek might've had of chasing us, for one thing," Montez said.

"We can outfly him! And we might've been able to lead him somewhere and then capture him! And all he has to do is think about it and another dino will show up. You didn't cancel anything!"

Montez shot her an annoyed glance over his shoulder. "You're yelling at me for killing a Confederate dino."

The shouts of men and clomping of boots on wooden gangplanks came from the campsite below. They hadn't spotted Magdalys and Montez yet, but it was only a matter of time. And having a loud brother-sister fight would only make it sooner.

She took a breath, lowered her voice to a severe growl. "I'm yelling at you because the man whose favorite mount you just sniped was talking five minutes ago about how he wants me dead, and now he thinks I did it and he wants me dead even more."

"Hold on, I can fix that problem too if I can spot him," Montez said, turning back to his rifle.

"You can't just shoot everything and think it's going to make the whole problem go away."

"It's worked for me so far."

"Montez!" She was shouting again, but she couldn't stop herself. "Stop making snappy comebacks and just listen to me!"

He let out a long breath, sat up on the branch. Turned to face her.

"The Knights of the Golden Circle are planning something. Something huge. They think they can clinch victory not just in this war but over the whole continent. The hemisphere! They'll take what the Confederacy's built and spread it across the world, a whole empire of slavery." That was how the nation she was fighting to protect had gotten its start too, Magdalys realized, but right now it was the only one standing in the way of an even greater threat, so she'd have to deal with that part later. "I need to stop them. *We* need to stop them. I can't do it alone."

Very slightly, Montez's face softened.

"If you take out Drek, they'll just get Crawbell or someone else to do it, but we won't have any idea who or what they're planning or anything else. But if we can figure out what they're up to, who their leadership is, where they get their money, then we can crush the whole organization and wipe them off the map for good."

Montez looked away. Down below, the men were yelling

back and forth about something; Magdalys couldn't make out their words.

"You haven't seen what I have," Montez said very quietly.

She nodded and sighed. "I know, Montez." *I'm sorry* didn't make sense. No words did.

"There are so many of them. And they just keep coming and coming and coming." He shook his head, sniffled. "Over the barricades and into the camp. And when you've seen that, when you've faced that, and felt *that* fear, as they rush up toward you and each and every one of them wants you dead or in chains, then you learn that you take whatever chance you can get to make their numbers smaller." He raised one shoulder, wiped his eyes. "That's all."

Magdalys didn't have anything to say back to that; she just wanted her brother to be okay. She wanted to shatter the whole world so they could rebuild it into one that loved them. She wanted to scream and cry without having to worry about giving away their position to soldiers who would murder them.

"And what happens when we give up a shot on Drek," Montez said, "and then he sends his dinos into battle and wipes out more of our troops? Or sends a T. rex rampaging through the streets of New Orleans? Aren't those deaths on us, Mags?"

"Just as much as the ones that'll happen when the Knights send the next wave of attacks against us, and the one after that. But no, none of those are on us, Montez, not really. They're on them. It just means we have to stop him. Stop all of them."

She turned, because her brother's sad eyes were about to make her break down, and headed for Dizz.

"We're just kids," Montez said behind her.

She nodded. "I know."

"This shouldn't be on us. We should be playing and worrying about our homework and what we're gonna be when we grow up."

"I know."

"Not how to take down slavery empires and whether or not to kill someone."

Magdalys grabbed the saddle straps and pulled herself up. She slid into position and looked at Montez. Steeled herself. "Let's go get Drek."

CHAPTER FOURTEEN
SEARCH AND ANNOY

CONFEDERATE TROOPS AND Bog Marauders swarmed through the forest as Magdalys and Montez flew silently above on Dizz's back. When he'd told her about what it felt like staring down so many of them in close quarters, she'd figured she would have that moment herself one day, but she never thought it would be just a few moments later.

They were everywhere — a sea of gray-and-brown jackets surging between trees and through swamps. And that meant one thing: The newly re-formed Army of the Mississippi was on the move.

"This is bad," Montez said, scanning the troops through his rifle scope.

"Where do you think they're headed?" They seemed to move in a hundred different directions at once, which probably meant they were looking for something. *Probably us*, Magdalys thought.

"I don't know, but our rendezvous point is straight ahead. Any sign of Drek?"

Magdalys shook her head. She'd been trying to catch sight of that bright red beard since they'd flown out over the forest. And now there were too many troops below to make much sense of. And anyway, they'd be spotted soon.

She swung Dizz off to the side where there were fewer soldiers down below and then dipped under the tree line and glided smoothly between the towering oaks.

"He's probably riding something," Magdalys said. "Maybe I can find him that way." She closed her eyes, trusting Dizz to keep them from crashing into anything, and inhaled a deep breath of thick, mulchy swamp air. What dinos were nearby?

Immediately, the *kree-kree* song of some small, fluttering reptile that Magdalys couldn't quite identify filled her. Whatever it was, it didn't seem like something Drek would choose as a mount.

What else?

A *brunk brunk brunk* noise rose up within. Something big, four-legged. A stego maybe. Now more of them. Had to be a convoy, part of the Confederate Army. Drek could be with them, but she doubted it, considering the argument he'd just had with their commanding officer. And marching along in a line like a regular battle grunt didn't seem like his style.

She opened her eyes and glanced around. No more

soldiers, just the flitting of dragonflies and gentle rustle of leaves and Spanish moss in the Louisiana wind.

Breeka! a familiar high-pitched voice crooned. *Breeka! Breeka!*

"Milo?" Magdalys gasped, swooping low with Dizz and glancing around.

"Where?" Montez asked.

"Somewhere up ahead."

"Hey!" someone yelled off to their left. "There she is!"

"Hold tight," Magdalys said, diving even lower and speeding up as a bullet thwunked into a nearby tree trunk.

"Get back here!"

They zoomed just above the forest floor, sweeping left and right between bushes and vines. More gunfire crackled around them.

"There!" Montez said, pointing up ahead.

Magdalys saw it: a flash of something white flapping around Milo's tiny running body. What did he have? She sent Dizz rocketing forward, under a trunk that had been nearly cut in half by a mortar shell and around a giant moss-covered mound.

"Units converge!" someone yelled. "Triple time!"

"Open fire!" another voice commanded from not far away.

"Grab him!" Magdalys yelled, coming up fast behind Milo as Montez leaned all the way to one side of the saddle and reached out his long arm.

"Got him!" Montez yelled, and Magdalys sent Dizz

hurtling skyward as tree branches cracked and collapsed around them beneath a withering barrage of musket shots.

Blam! Blamblamblamblam! Blam blam! Blam! Gunfire took over the forest, became the world. Dizz hurled up, up, up, bursting out of the canopy and into the open sky.

"Wooooooooooo!!" Magdalys yelled as they flew clear of the trees and away. She was terrified and heartbroken, surrounded by enemies, but at least for this escapade, they'd survived, against all odds. "Everyone okay?"

"I'm good," Montez reported. "So's Milo. Also, he seems to have snagged a present for us in his travels."

That must've been whatever the flapping white shape around him was. "Oh?" Magdalys pointed Dizz toward their rendezvous spot.

"Looks like a bunch of boring stuff about migrational patterns of different dinos across North America. Numbers, numbers, charts, blah, blah, blah. What is it? Why are you looking at me like that?"

Magdalys had slowly turned around in the saddle and was staring wide-eyed at Montez. She looked down at Milo, who was sitting in his lap looking very satisfied with himself.

"Montez," she said. "That's the . . . Those are . . ."

"Speak, sis!"

"THOSE ARE THE SECRET DOCUMENTS THE GRANDMASTER GAVE TO DREK SO HE COULD COMPLETE HIS MISSION!!"

"Whoa, now."

"THE ONE THAT THEY THINK WILL BRING THEM VICTORY AND WIPE US OFF THE MAP!! MONTEZ!!"

"Mags, you're yelling. Like a lot. But also whoa! Are you sure?"

She took the papers. "They gotta be!"

Breeka! Milo chirped, still very pleased.

Numbers and charts spilled across page after page within the loosely bound folder. Milo must've sensed her wanting to get her hands on it somehow and just . . . made a dash. Either that or there was some other dinowrangler with her abilities nearby who also wanted it, but that didn't seem possible. One way or another, it was hers now. Making heads or tails of it would be a whole other problem, but she'd worry about that when she was safely back in . . .

"Uh," Montez said. "Looks like we're showing up right on time."

Magdalys glanced up from the documents.

In an open stretch of marsh along the bayou, a giant toad stood at its full height, towering over the tall grass. Colonel Wolfgang Hands waved from between its eyes. "Hey, how do you drive these things?" he yelled. "We gotta get out of here!" Bijoux was beside him, prepping weapons, while Grappler looked on from a little farther back.

Mapper and Tom circled up above on Beans.

In front of them, six trikes marched side by side across the swamplands, attached by a massive steel harness. Each had a howitzer attached to the armor on either flank. Briggs and Toussaint rode the two in the middle. "You made it!" Toussaint called. "Yeeeeeehaw!"

"RECONNAISSANCE!!" Briggs hollered, throwing a fist into the air.

"Ahh, speaking of reconnaissance," Montez said. "Don't look behind us."

She did.

The whole forest rustled and rumbled with the movement of many, many dinos and men through the trees. That scattered rush they'd seen before had solidified into a single, unflinching focus. At the far end of what must've been several miles of the Confederate Army, a command sauropod gazed out over the canopy toward the east. The march to reconquer New Orleans had begun.

CHAPTER FIFTEEN
SKIRT THE EDGE AND SURGE

"**A**AAAAAAAAAAAAAAAAAAAAHHHH!!!!!!!"
Montez yelled as they hurtled on toadback over trees and a whole battalion of trikeriders.

Magdalys just tried to stay low and make sure her rifle was ready. The toad's skin was slimy and bumpy, and she felt like any wrong move or gust of wind might send her flying over the side, and then, if the fall didn't kill her, the enemy soldiers definitely would.

KA-FWOM!!! The whole earth shook as they landed on a muddy embankment and immediately the *crack, crack* of rifles started up from below. "Didn't waste any time, did they?" Mapper growled, taking up position behind one of the toad's big lumpy growths.

"You probably wouldn't either if an amphibian the size of a hotel dropped out of the sky on your army," Wolfgang said, flattening himself against the slimy dome and aiming into the clearing dust below.

Magdalys squinted, but all she saw were tiny flashes in the brown murk. A few bullets whizzed past, but they all went wide by a long shot. The soldiers below probably couldn't see much more than she could and were just taking desperate pot-shots. She raised her carbine.

There wasn't much of a plan, mostly because they didn't have many options. Wolfgang explained that the two other toads had wandered off together; he didn't want to speculate as to why. That meant they had one giant toad, six trikes, three dactyls (one injured), a microraptor, and eight soldiers to get past an entire army and make it to New Orleans in time to warn them of the impending attack. And Mapper was positive there were no shortcuts to be found — he'd closed his eyes and gone into a kind of trance, then shook his head. "Nothing that will get us there before them, anyway."

They'd talked about splitting up, but as dire as things were, they couldn't spare any firepower — even as it was, they'd probably be overrun pretty quickly.

The Confederates had spread their army across a wide swath of land and were marching forward in attack formation instead of a long narrow line. Wolfgang said it was in case they bumped into Banks's forces; this way they wouldn't have to scramble to get in position. "Just means we hit their farthest flank." He'd pointed to the very edge of their battle line, where a single squad of trikeriders marched through an open field a ways away from the main body of troops. "Drop a toad on 'em and cause enough chaos so they're distracted while our trikes are rolling up."

And that was exactly what they'd done.

Bang! screamed Magdalys's carbine. *Bang! Bang! Bang!* Every time she saw a muzzle flash below, she aimed for it. She had no idea if she hit anything or not, just that between her, Wolfgang, Bijoux, and Montez, and with Mapper and Tom shooting from dactylback, they should be able to lay down enough fire to at least send the Confederates into a temporary flurry of confusion.

Fwiiiiiii a bullet sang as it sped past, a little too close for comfort.

Magdalys hunkered lower and let off two shots at where she thought it had come from.

It was only yesterday that she'd (probably) taken her first life in battle. Who could really tell in the thick of things? Bog Marauders had been attacking and she'd pointed her carbine and shot and shot, and men had fallen screaming from their sinornith mounts into the swamp, but Mapper had been shooting too and maybe they'd lived and —

THWUMP!! A bullet landed in the toad's thick flesh beside her and Magdalys jumped back, heart racing wildly in her ears. She couldn't afford to get lost in her thoughts like that, not with enemy fire coming in all around her. It was a good thing the toad didn't seem to mind getting shot much. He turned his monstrous yellow eyes downward to the troops massing below, and Magdalys felt his whole body convulse as that freight-train-sized tongue unraveled itself from his open mouth and flashed out. An armored triceratops squealed, lifted suddenly into the air, and then the toad's enormous mouth closed around it, and for a moment there was just awed silence.

"Yaaaaaaaa!!" Mapper yelled from where Beans was flying up above, and then the shooting started up again.

"Here they come!" Wolfgang called, nodding at the woods behind them, where Toussaint and Briggs were wrangling their six trikes in a mad dash toward the skirmish.

"They got reinforcements headed our way," Tom warned from Dizz's back, just as the dactyl spun a wild loop-de-loop through the clouds above. "Whoa! Dizz, slow down, man! Can't make out what's coming! Dizz!"

Time to cause some trouble, Magdalys thought, lowering her carbine. "Montez, cover me." He scurried over to where she crouched, almost slipping along the way, then got into position and let off a few shots into the fray.

Magdalys tried to focus. About ten enemy trikes stomped around below. And Tom was right: There were more dinos on the way, but Magdalys couldn't make out what they were yet. She'd deal with them when they got here.

For now, she had some trikes to upset. It wouldn't take

much pushing, probably. The toad had already gotten them riled up nicely for her. She reached out, immediately linking with five of them. A mess of frantic triceratops grunts and pants rose up within her: *Garunga garunga . . . bah . . . bah . . . garunga . . .*

Magdalys sent two of them charging into a third and the other three spinning in widening circles as troops scattered and were tossed to either side.

"Impressive," Wolfgang said, walking up beside her and blinking his one eye down at the chaos below.

"Bog Marauders incoming," Mapper called. "Sinorniths on your ten."

Magdalys glanced up, narrowed her eyes. These were the same guys who had chased her and Mapper through the Atchafalaya and trapped Montez and the others in that mansion for days on end. She sent a half dozen careening out of the sky with a wave of her hand. The others landed quickly and launched back up, but farther away, hoping to get out of range.

"Uh, Private Magdalys," Wolfgang said. He was squinting through the spyglass, gritting his teeth. "There's, ah . . . You should see this."

"What?" She took the retractable metal cylinder, peered through. Nothing made sense. Dinos were tossing their riders and scurrying in a fevered circle. Most of them were trikes, plus a whole squadron of ankys and a slew of raptors. Men yelled, trying to wrangle their mounts back into some kind of order. The dinos paid them no mind. At first Magdalys thought they were turning back — had something happened? Then she heard a voice carried along on the warm bayou wind: "For Sweet Virginiaaa!" All at once, the dinos turned toward Magdalys and fell into formation.

Then they charged.

CHAPTER SIXTEEN
GET AWAY

"**I**F YOU SEE Drek," Magdalys said, nudging her brother, "take the shot."

"Huh?" He swung his rifle around, scanning the oncoming surge of dinos. "What happened to getting information and there's bigger things at play than the one guy and all that?"

She shook her head. "Change of plans." The dinos were still out of her reach, but they wouldn't be for long. And then . . . she'd never wrangled that many at once before. There had to be at least thirty-five, maybe forty. Back at Chickamauga, Elizabeth Crawbell had probably had even more than that in her archaeopteryx squad, but they were small and seemed to have been trained for those kinds of formation attacks. These were random battle dinos, and Drek had forced them under his will and sent them all together like a bristling, stomping outpouring of his rage at Magdalys for killing Sweet Virginia.

And she hadn't done it!

But Drek had already had it out for her, even before Montez took out his precious crimson dactyl. He'd seen what she could do, been bested by her, and now he'd leveled up himself, fueled by a homicidal wrath with one singular focus.

"We have to make a run for it," Magdalys said.

"I'm not sure if —" Wolfgang started.

"I can't hold them off!" Panic seized her. "I can't! Not all at once! Not that many!" A headlong dash for safety was the only option. They had to run and they had to go now if they were going to have any chance of making it. Drek would wear out every dino in his reach to destroy Magdalys, of that she was sure.

"Private Mapper!" Wolfgang hollered. "Private Summers! Get down here, boys! Make it snappy!"

Ka-bang!! Montez's rifle blasted.

Magdalys jumped. "Did you see him? Did you get him?"

"No," Montez said. *Ka-bang!! Bang! Bang!* "It's the Marauders — they're coming back. Or at least" — he gazed through his sight again — "their mounts are."

Magdalys spun around. Out in the sky, a flurry of sinorniths sailed toward them in what looked like slow motion, those death-dealing jaws open wide.

"We're here, sir!" Mapper reported, landing Beans on the toad's head behind them. Dizz came skittering down with Tom a second later.

"It's me that he wants," Magdalys said. "We have to split up. He'll . . . We have to split up."

"Private Bijoux," Wolfgang said. "Tell our boys with the trikes to make a break for it. Cover them from above. Head straight for New Orleans and don't turn around for nothing."

Bang, bang! Montez's rifle crowed behind them and sinorniths plummeted screeching through the sky.

Magdalys unslung her shoulder bag and handed it to Mapper. "Take this," she said. "We stole some documents from the Knights of the Golden Circle. It's all in here. Whatever they're up to, it's in these papers. Get it to New Orleans, Mapper. You have to."

Mapper furrowed his brow. "I don't want to leave you behind . . . The . . . the squad, Mags . . ."

He was right. The Dactyl Hill Squad had been shattered by this war, and somehow it felt like that sacred bond would be forever broken if they separated. But there was nothing else to be done. She steeled her face. "Go. You have to. Get these documents to General Banks. I'll . . . I'll be okay."

He hugged her so suddenly and fiercely that Magdalys almost burst into tears. "Go!" she ordered, wriggling out of his grasp and blinking furiously.

Ka-blam BLAM!!

"They're almost on us!" Montez yelled.

Mapper took one last look at Magdalys, then threw her satchel over his shoulder and ran off, clambering onto Beans in a single leap and took off into the air behind Dizz and Bijoux.

The last thing she saw was Milo's tiny head peeking out of the satchel and staring after her.

Wolfgang was beside Montez, firing off shot after shot at the sinorniths circling above. There were too many. And a whole other attack coming from the ground. And Drek somewhere nearby, controlling it all.

She held up both hands, trying to calm her frantic mind.

JUHJUHJUHJUHJUHJUHJUH came the urgent burble of the toad beneath her.

Jump! Magdalys thought. *Go!* But even as he crouched to leap, three sinorniths landed on one leg, each sinking their venomous jaws into his flank.

"No!" Magdalys yelled.

JUH!

She swung her arm, and the sinorniths stumbled some, looking around. *Be gone!* she thought. They looked up at her, and then a *ka-blam!* cracked out and one fell away squawking.

"What's wrong?" Wolfgang asked, loading more cartridges into his rifle.

The other two sinorniths leapt.

Ka-blam! Blam! Wolfgang blasted away one of them, and Magdalys finally reached the other and sent it scurrying off.

JUHJUHJUHJUHJUHJUH!! the toad warbled.

"The sinorniths bit our toad," Magdalys said. "And I don't know . . . I don't know if it can withstand their venom."

Jump! she thought. *Please!*

The horde of dinos was upon them, just a few feet away.

The toad crouched low again, sprang up but not as high as it had been. They flew through the air. Montez yelped and stumbled, almost toppling down the slippery, wart-covered hide.

"Montez!" Magdalys reached out, but he'd already pulled himself up and rolled over onto his back, panting. His rifle had sailed over the side.

And then they were crashing through the treetops, coming to a sloppy, collapsed landing not nearly far enough away from the storming dinos.

"You alright?" Wolfgang asked, passing his sidearm to Montez.

"Yeah, but . . ."

"Doesn't matter," the corporal huffed. "We use what we got."

Already, Drek's dinos were bearing down on them once again.

"I don't know what to do," Magdalys said.

"We gotta jump again," Wolfgang said. "We'll do our best to hold 'em off."

Bang! Bang! Bang! Montez let loose with a pistol in each hand. The screams of dinos sounded nearby amidst the thunder of their approach.

C'mon, toad, Magdalys urged. *I know you're hurt, but . . . we gotta get out of here, buddy. We gotta go. We gotta live. C'mon!*

Juhjuhjuhjuhjuhjuh came the murky reply, now diminished somehow, that poison working its way through the massive, ancient creature. He stirred though, turned, and hopped a little ways forward, then again. Magdalys climbed to the top of his now bowed head and gazed out across the wilderness. There. Up ahead, a lake stretched out into the distance toward New Orleans. And there on the far shore: the sharp incline of a battlement wall, where Magdalys could just make out the shiny black lengths of those ten-gallon cannons called Parrott rifles poking out. Above them, the stars and stripes of the US flag waved in the wind.

We just gotta make it to the water, she thought. *See? We'll be safe there. C'mon, ol' boy!*

Beneath her, the toad shivered, then leapt half-heartedly again.

Blam! Blam! Blam!

Juhjuhjuhjuhjuhjuh, the toad sighed.

Blam!

C'mon, buddy!

And then another sound came to her — the sweet familiar *fubba fubba* of one of her favorite pteros. In all the frenzy of battle and escape, she'd forgotten that Grappler was still with them, curled up in a secluded area of the toad, nursing her wounds. Now the dactyl sang a sweet song of *fubba*s within Magdalys, and the toad seemed to answer in kind: *Juhjuhjuh juhjuhjuh.*

"Yes, girl," Magdalys whispered. "Tell him we gotta make it to the water. Come on!"

The toad leapt.

JuhJUH juhJUH juhJUH it sang, now even more animated.

It leapt again, a little farther this time. The lake was only a few more jumps away. Mountainous clouds cluttered the sky above as darkness began to creep around the edges of the world.

They leapt again, even farther this time, but still with a woozy kind of sloppiness.

Fubba fubba fubba!

The toad broke into an awkward kind of stumble toward the water. Behind them, the dinos still clamored along in furious pursuit, but they were a little ways back now.

The toad took two more galloping, floppy struts and then crouched low and launched into the air, sailing clear out over the water.

"YEAAAAAAH!!" Magdalys yelled, but then her eyes went wide. Two fizzling crackles of light streaked directly toward them from the far shore. The low booms reached her a moment later. Artillery fire. But that was a Union outpost!

Swerve! Magdalys pleaded, a second too late.

"Incoming!" Wolfgang yelled.

The first shell shrieked over their heads and then erupted into a blinding flash of light as it burst across the sky. Magdalys dove for cover, shrapnel shredding her arms and back, and then felt her stomach plummet as they went into free fall toward the lake.

BABANGAAA!!!! The other shell burst nearby them, more shrapnel and the sky spinning wild circles and the dark waters of the lake rushing up, up, up to greet them as the toad warbled his desperate, dying song through Magdalys: *Juh . . . juh . . . juhhhhhh.*

PART TWO

CHAPTER SEVENTEEN
AWASH

A **DARKNESS DEEPER THAN** any Magdalys had ever known covered the world. Giant walls of movement swayed and swooshed around her; she felt each tiny and humongous twitch of the universe.

And a murky silence prevailed, broken by a few faraway burbles and rumblings.

There was no time, no distance, no past or present.

And then: *JUH!!*

Two enormous yellow eyes opened up in the void.

JuhJUH!

I thought you were dead, Magdalys thought to her immense and ancient friend. She felt so happy and sad at the same time. Cannons boomed somewhere far away, a whole other realm, it felt like.

I'm so sorry I failed you.

Juhjuhjuh, the toad replied, and it felt like a laughing rebuke. She hadn't failed him, the toad insisted. He had gone along with her knowing full well what the risks were, that these tiny, strange mammals were at war, had been for some time, in one form or another. Magdalys had been a pleasant reminder that sometimes you have to stand up and fight. *Can't just sleep in the mud for an entire lifetime, right?*

Magdalys had no idea how she understood all this, but it was as clear as a glass of water what he was saying in her mind. The toad let out a tremendous *juh*-inflected chortle and then narrowed his huge eyes on her. *You must live. There is still work to do. I will heal. You don't worry about me.*

The darkness swirled.

Magdalys felt herself rising, rising, pushing through the void, up, up, up toward the surface and then with a gasp she collapsed onto a shoreline as the emptiness slipped from her amidst the toad's far-off chuckles. She crawled away from the splish of tiny waves, leaned over, and then vomited up what felt like a whole gallon of lake water.

She coughed, wiped her mouth, then rolled onto her back, panting, and stared at the darkening sky.

How much time had passed? Where were the others? She tried to get up, couldn't.

"Hey!" someone yelled nearby. "There's another! C'mon!"

What side of the lake had the toad dropped her off on?

Terror swept over her. She rolled her head to one side, tried to make out who the approaching soldiers were, but in the dim twilight it was impossible to tell blue from gray.

"You there!" one of them yelled, holding up his sidearm and breaking into a run toward her.

Magdalys closed her eyes. There was no way she could escape; she couldn't even stand. But maybe there was a dino nearby . . .

Rough hands grabbed her and pulled her to her feet. "What are you doing here, girl? Who are you with?"

Who was she with? What were they talking about?

She stumbled, shaking her head, the whole world a blurry mess of dark trees and the gentle lapping of the lake. "C'mon, get a move on!"

She had to run. Whoever these men were, they weren't friendly. They wouldn't keep her safe. They might capture or kill her. She had to . . . She took two feeble steps, tripped, and collapsed into the mud, coughing.

"Hey! What's the matter with you, girl? Get her up! C'mon, then!"

The hands that clenched tight to either one of Magdalys's arms didn't care about her. She wasn't a person to them, just a broken object that might hurt them, might be useful somehow, but mostly was just a nuisance. They yanked her to her feet and shoved her forward into a stumbling walk.

"Take her to the general," one said. "That's where the

others are. Maybe we'll make sense out of what happened tonight."

The others, Magdalys thought. At least, wherever she was going, some of her friends would be there. She stilled the raging storm inside herself and walked forward through the gathering night.

CHAPTER EIGHTEEN

THE VERY . . . WELL, THE VERY SOMETHING GENERAL BANKS

THEY LED MAGDALYS through a dim, scattered campsite to an elaborate tent with soldiers standing guard out front.

"Found another contraband," one of the men who'd captured her said.

Contraband. That was the word they used to describe people who had escaped from slavery and made their way to the Union lines. Up above, the American flag seemed to preside over the campsite. Magdalys exhaled. So she hadn't been snatched by the enemy, at least, although she sure didn't feel like she was with friends either.

"That's what I'm trying to tell you!" a familiar voice said from inside the tent.

"Mapper!" Magdalys yelled, shrugging off the men's heavy hands on her shoulders and making a break for the entranceway.

"Mags?" Mapper called. "You're alive!"

The guards stepped in front of her, blocking her way. "Ho there, girl."

"Let me through!" Magdalys demanded. "Mapper!"

"Sir!" Wolfgang's gruff voice boomed. "That is a member of my troop! I demand you allow her entrance."

A sullen pause filled the air.

"A girl," a quiet voice said, "a member of your troop, Corporal Hands? I don't recall the United States Army allowing women to serve in our ranks, let alone Negro ones."

"General Banks, sir," Wolfgang insisted. "I can explain everything. Please."

"Very well," Banks said. "Bring her in."

The guards stepped back, and Magdalys ran through the tent flaps and stood panting in an elaborate office, lit on all sides by flickering lanterns. General Banks sat in a fancy wooden chair at the far end, his feet propped up on the table tortoise. He was a middle-aged man with plain brown hair, a plain brown mustache, and a plain, indistinguishable face. If he ever committed a crime, Magdalys thought, the only thing a witness would be able to say about him was that he was a regular white guy with a mustache. There was simply nothing else to report. He raised one eyebrow at Magdalys, looking, quite simply, bored out of his mind. "What exactly are you supposed to be?" Banks asked.

Mapper, Montez, Wolfgang, Tom Summers, Toussaint, Briggs, and Bijoux stood at attention in front of the general. They looked bedraggled and exhausted, and some of them were soaking wet like Magdalys was, but they were alive! They'd made it! And Mapper had her satchel slung over one shoulder. She wanted to hug each of them with all her might, but she knew it wasn't the time for that.

"Major General, sir," Magdalys pleaded, "the Confederates are massing for an attack! You have to —"

"I literally don't *have* to do anything at all," he scoffed. "Do you think you get to give orders here?"

"No, I —"

"You know who does get to give orders here?"

"Sir, if you'd just —"

"I do!" Banks huffed. "That's it. I give orders. Now, I asked you a direct question and I expect an answer to that question and not a single word that is not an answer to that question. Is that clear?"

Fighting down the burst of anger within her, Magdalys tightened her lips and nodded. "I'm . . . Ma . . . Private Magdalys Roca, sir!" She snapped a salute.

"Reeeeally?" Banks stood, cocked his head at her. "How fascinating. What makes you think you're allowed to serve in *my* army, I wonder?"

She shouldn't have said *private*. She wasn't sure what rank General Grant's offer made her exactly, but it was more than a foot soldier. "I'm part of a newly created top secret special division, sir. Brought in by General Grant. He asked me to run it, really. So, I'm not technically part of your army, exactly. Sir." That came out ruder than she'd meant it to. "But, sir —"

Banks, who had been bemusedly studying the far corner of the command tent, whirled on her. "Excuse me?"

"I meant —"

"You would like me to believe, young lady, that the high commander of the combined United States military forces saw fit to create a *secret special* unit" — he crinkled up his face as he said it, making it abundantly clear he didn't buy one word she said — "and put a little Negro child in charge of it, hm?"

"Yes, I ha —"

"And what is it, exactly, that qualifies you to be the head of this super secret special division, hm?"

"I have a letter from General Grant that explains everything." She reached into her jacket pocket, pulled out the soaked, crinkled parchment, and unfolded it. Her heart sank.

"A letter from General Grant that explains everything," Banks parroted. "How amusing."

Except she didn't, not anymore. All Magdalys had was a soggy scrap of paper with faded ink stains splotched across it. The lake water had destroyed her one piece of proof of what she said.

"Is that your little letter?" Banks asked.

Magdalys shook her head as the tent seemed to close in on her. "It's . . . But . . ."

"General Banks, sir!" Montez barked. "This is my si —"

"I don't remember giving you permission to speak, Private," Banks snapped.

"Permission to speak, General Banks?" Wolfgang said.

Banks nodded.

"I saw the letter myself, sir. The child is telling the truth."

"And who are you" — Banks peered at Wolfgang's uniform — "Corporal?"

"We don't have time for this!" Magdalys yelled. "The Confederates are about to mount an attack! You have to stop them!"

"It's true!" Mapper said. "She's not lying!"

Banks shook his head. "Take her away," he snarled, and heavy hands wrapped once again around Magdalys's arms, yanking her backward.

"No!" she yelled. "Let me go!"

"And send out the scouts," Banks added grudgingly as Magdalys was dragged out the door. "Find out what all this mess is about."

CHAPTER NINETEEN
DETAINED

EVERYTHING WAS WET and dripping and the thick swampiness covered the dingy room like a nasty moist blanket, and mosquitoes and that endless dripping and the sound of sloshing water nearby — the bayou or the lake or whatever it was just kept sloshing — and the trinkling song of some stream too, and the drips and more mosquitoes and heat and near darkness, it just didn't end, any of it, it just went on and on and on forever into the night.

Magdalys slumped onto the rickety wooden bench — the only bit of furniture in the old shack they'd shoved her in. Probably a boathouse, she figured, eyeing the pulleys, hooks, and ropes dangling in the darkness above. Or maybe something much creepier . . .

She shook off the growing sense of dread. Stood up. Sat back down. Rolled her eyes.

There were most likely dinos nearby. It was a Union outpost, after all. They had to have some mounts. But she didn't even have it in her to concentrate and try to find them. What was the point? She was a prisoner of her own army. Captured by the people who were supposed to be the good guys. Captured, humiliated, and locked in a creepy murder shack. Or boathouse. Or whatever.

And what had happened to her dactyls?

Dizz and Beans were probably alright. She hadn't had time to ask Mapper or Bijoux about them, but she felt like they would've tried to say something if anything had happened. Right? But Grappler . . . Grappler, who had saved Magdalys's life more than once since they'd left New York and even when wounded had managed to help encourage the toad to get them to safety. Grappler, who might not be able to swim . . .

Magdalys was pacing and she hadn't even realized she'd stood up.

Maybe the toad helped Grappler just like he'd helped Magdalys.

Maybe.

And anyway, the Confederates would launch their attack at any moment and none of this would matter, because this puny Union outpost would be overrun and New Orleans taken and then whatever Emperor Maximilian was plotting with the

French in Mexico would go down unimpeded and their armies would all join forces to create that massive slavery empire the Knights of the Golden Circle were so excited about. And — Magdalys smacked her own forehead — those secret documents Milo had stolen for her! She'd told Mapper to give them to General Banks, but Banks would probably just destroy them or forget about them; he'd never believe that a devastating plot was afoot.

Magdalys's pacing had brought her in front of the door. She had to do something. But what? Nothing made sense. There were no right answers, and all the people she trusted were either scattered across this war-torn world or in the same predicament as her. Or dead.

She raised her fist to bang on the wooden planks, and the door swung open.

"Whoa!" Magdalys said.

"Whoa!" Mapper said, his face lit by torchlight.

A white soldier stood behind him, frowning severely. "In." The soldier shoved Mapper unceremoniously through the door and then slammed it.

Magdalys wrapped around him and sniffed once, then simply burst into tears. He smelled like swamp and dirt, but he also smelled like Mapper, which meant, in a weird sort of way, like home. It was strange to think of the time Magdalys had spent at the orphanage as peaceful, but compared to what she'd been through over the past couple of months, New York seemed like a whole other life.

Mapper was crying too. She felt his little hiccuped sobs against her shoulder; they mixed with her own. Neither needed to explain their tears, they'd been through it all together, fought off the panic and frenzy of battle, the terror of being about to die at any given moment, the thrill of surviving another day when it seemed like the whole world wanted to kill you.

When there was no more crying to do, Magdalys and Mapper sat beside each other on the bench and shook their heads in the darkness.

"I think the breaking point for me," Mapper said, wiping his nose, "was being captured and roughed up by our own team."

Magdalys nodded. "That was mine too. If I'd known what a useless doofus Banks was gonna be, I never would've told you to give those secret Golden Circle documents to him."

"What, these?" Mapper lifted his shirt where, instead of the dark brown of his skin, Magdalys saw the yellowish beige of parchment paper.

She leapt up. "Mapper, you genius! How did you — What did you — ?"

He made a figure eight with his head, raising one eyebrow and shrugging his shoulders. "I had a feeling that guy wasn't gonna be trustworthy, just from the way the soldiers from the 9th talked about him. So I stashed 'em here just in case. And lo and behold, my hunch was correct!"

"Mapper, you are the greatest!"

"Yeah, thanks to me, when the Knights take over the whole world, we'll already know their secret plan, so that's cool."

He chuckled, and so did Magdalys, and then they were both laughing hysterically and neither knew exactly why, except everything had become so horrible and absurd and terrifying at the same time, and even their allies couldn't be trusted and nothing made any sense.

When the door flew open and two soldiers stomped in, Mapper and Magdalys had slid down to the floor in wild giggle fits.

"TEN-HUT!" one of the soldiers barked, and they did their best to get themselves together, finally making it off the floor and into some semblance of standing at attention by the time General Banks walked in, looking extremely put out around that mediocre mustache.

Magdalys and Mapper saluted, both of them still panting and sweating and bedraggled in almost every way.

"Well!" General Banks snorted.

"Sir, yes sir!" Mapper yelled, and then Magdalys spat out an uncontrollable guffaw through lips squeezed so tight together they made it sound exactly like a pterofart.

That did both of them back in: Any semblance of having it together was splattered, and they both fell out laughing once again.

"This is the child I'm supposed to believe General Grant has entrusted an entire top secret division of the United States Armed Forces to?" Banks mused. "How interesting."

Magdalys sobered her expression quickly as anger and

shame duked it out inside her. How could she have ruined that letter? Especially when she was within the clutches of such a senseless dullard! "He did, sir!" she insisted, hating the pleading tone in her own voice. "I swear he did!"

"It's true," Mapper said, finally calming down too.

Banks waved them off. "That's lovely, children. I didn't come here to rehash this argument though, which you've already lost, anyway."

Magdalys tried not to slump.

"However!" Banks arched an eyebrow. "I sent out an elite mounted scout unit to scour the nearby swamplands."

An elite mounted scout unit, Magdalys thought. *How cool* . . . She wondered what they'd ridden. It would have to be something fast, of course, but also amphibious and skilled at complicated maneuvers, because the forest terrain was so swampy. A lot of the fast-moving dinos were better on plains and drier landscapes.

"I decided, since you all seemed so convinced of your discovery and since some of the reconnaissance collected by your little group was actually quite precise, to double-check the data."

Magdalys hoped the general had said as much to the men and that Briggs was there to hear it — it would make his whole day!

"As it turns out," Banks continued, "there are indeed indications of a sizable force massing at the far side of the lake." He said it like it was just another update in this long ridiculous life, not a direct threat to his entire army. But maybe, Magdalys reasoned, imminent destruction was just another daily event during wartime.

He also said it like it was actually true for the first time, like *he* was the one telling *them* something new, not confirming what they'd seen with their own eyes. It made Magdalys want to spit. She took a deep breath and swallowed back all the sarcasm she wanted to let loose on him.

"Um, we know that!" Mapper snipped. "We barely escaped them alive!"

Magdalys did her best not to fall out laughing again.

"Well, now it's officially confirmed!" Banks retorted. "By official US military sources!"

"What are the Louisiana 9th?" Magdalys said. "Hired mercenaries?"

"Young lady!" Banks growled.

No, Magdalys realized. *The Louisiana 9th are black. That's why their intelligence doesn't count.* When Banks had said *official US military sources*, what he'd really meant were *white* ones.

"And what are we?" Mapper demanded. "Dinopoop?"

Banks rounded on them. "That's the point I was trying to get to and am already regretting!"

"What?" Magdalys and Mapper said together.

"I had decided to delay our westerly march until next year, for reasons, and that appears to have been the prudent decision. *However!* We can't have threats on the outskirts of our city, you know. *Since* your intelligence has proven to be useful."

He paused, glanced away with a frown. "Potentially crucial, even, to the survival of our southern army."

"Sir, yes sir!" Mapper agreed enthusiastically.

"And since the soldiers of the Louisiana 9th vouched for you both and swore you'd mustered in under their watch and were competent, distinguished even, under fire —"

"They said that?" Magdalys said.

"Stop interrupting me or I promise I will take back what I'm about to say before I even say it!" Banks barked.

"Sir, yes sir!" Magdalys and Mapper said.

"Because of all that, and in spite of everything else including my better judgment, I've decided to allow you to remain in my army as privates."

He really said it like he was doing them a favor, Magdalys marveled. She supposed it was better than the alternative. She still planned on dismantling the Knights of the Golden Circle, one way or another, and being forced out of the Union Army almost as soon as she'd joined wouldn't be a great start. Plus, Banks had sounded like she might have even more dire consequences to face if things had turned out another way . . .

"You are to report to the French Quarter barracks in the morning and receive your assignments," Banks said. "Is that clear, children?"

"Sir, yes sir!"

"And there will be no more talk of top secret units or General Grant!"

Magdalys bristled. "But —"

"*This* is how you will be of service to your country, privates. Not by playing make-believe and living in a land of fairy tales. Don't make me regret my decision," Banks warned, turning on his heel and marching out of the room. "If that happens, I'll make sure you regret it more than I do."

He slammed the door.

CHAPTER TWENTY
POOP DUTY

"**A**SSIGNMENTS!" MAGDALYS HUFFED for the eight hundred and fifty-sixth time as she poured another bucket of water across the stable floors. "If this is the real way for us to be of service to our country —"

"Then the country must be way more full of dinopoop than you'd thought," Mapper finished for her. He started making his way over the uneven stone with a push mop, shoving the last bits of narstiness to either side. There was still dried poop crusted to the floor that they'd have to chip away at with shovels when this part was done.

"Wow, steal my thunder why don't you," Magdalys grunted.

"It'd be harder to steal if you didn't repeat it every day for two weeks straight."

Had it been two weeks already? Time had seemed to move

so slowly on poop duty, and there were no weekends to help keep track. The weather swung woozily back and forth between obscenely hot to downright chilly, and huge bugs and random swamp dinos wandered around freely, as if they owned the city of New Orleans, not the Union or Confederacy or Spanish or French or any other silly humans.

Magdalys hadn't had much of a chance to get out and see the city — she spent almost all day every day scrubbing the stables — but the glimpses she'd gotten and the stories she'd heard made her desperate to wander freely. It smelled like the swamps but a little fresher, with that sea breeze coming in from the gulf. Plus, someone was always baking bread or making coffee nearby. And at night, the streets of the French Quarter filled with revelers and the air seemed to tingle with the scents of all kinds of spicy cuisines simmering in pots.

"I hate everything," she grumbled.

"How do you think I feel?" Mapper said. "We're in a strange city, and I haven't even had a chance to survey the terrain, not really! And from what I have seen, it doesn't match the official maps! Which means!" He waved his hands around, exasperated.

"Which means there are new maps to be made!" Magdalys finished for him. They'd been doing a lot of finishing each other's sentences these days, even when it wasn't something they'd been repeating over and over for two weeks.

At least the dactyls were all okay. Dizz and Beans had indeed come in with their riders, and Grappler had shown up at the outpost a little after Magdalys, still struggling to fly and soaking wet but very much alive. General Banks had agreed to let them stay in the stables with the other battle mounts, seeing as how they'd provided an invaluable service to their country, etc. etc.

"I just feel like . . ." Magdalys said, not sure what she felt like yet but needing to get it off her chest anyway, ". . . liiiike . . ."

"Like if you don't do something more substantial than shovel dinopoop soon, you're going to explode," Mapper said.

That was it. That was it exactly.

Magdalys sighed, nodded. "We've come so far. And we still haven't had time to figure out whatever it is Drek and the Knights are up to! And the city is probably about to get attacked at any moment!" Last they'd heard, Banks had assigned several trike and raptor divisions, including what was left of the 9th, to the far western outpost. The Confederates had taken the hint and fallen back some, but who knew how long that would last.

Montez had sent a dactylgram to say they were all fine and back to target practice and goofing off during free time, and Magdalys had felt a twinge of jealousy that they were already back in the action and having fun while she and Mapper were . . .

"Poop alert!" Mapper yelled. The air got thick with that gnarly sulfur smell and then Magdalys heard the telltale *plop plop* of one of the stegos letting its breakfast go. She rolled her eyes. Not again! They had *just* gotten the main floor cleaned up.

"Can't you mind-meld with them and tell them not to poop or whatever," Mapper groaned. He swung open the gate to let the stego out of its enclosure and passed Magdalys a shovel.

"Then they'd just fill up with poop," she said.

"Right, then we could send 'em into the Confederate camp and they'd poop all over them!"

Magdalys snorted, and the snort turned into a giggle, and pretty soon they'd fallen back into yet another fit of laughter. This one was also interrupted by the sudden entrance of an officer — fortunately it wasn't General Banks this time though.

"At ease!" Lieutenant Franz Lietenwurst said, stepping in and saluting. Magdalys and Mapper hadn't gotten much better at jumping to attention out of a giggle fit, so they were both relieved that the most laid-back commander in their unit had been the one to show up. "Well," he said, surveying them, "I see you're already at ease. Very well. Listen, privates, I have some good news."

Magdalys wasn't even sure what that meant these days. She tried not to scowl at all the dim possibilities of what the US Army considered good news.

"Congress has finally passed the bill guaranteeing you equal pay."

"What?" Mapper gaped.

Magdalys just blinked. Black soldiers were paid a fraction

of what their white counterparts received, and most of them, including Magdalys and Mapper and all their friends in the 9th, had opted to refuse pay until they were equally compensated. It was relatively easy for Magdalys and Mapper — they ate in the mess hall and slept in the barracks, so they didn't have much need for money. Some of the other soldiers were supporting whole families back home though, and anyway the whole thing stank! But this . . . this meant that they'd won! They could get their pay and have some sense of equality in the ranks too!

"I can only say," Franz went on, "I'm sorry it took so long." He shook his head. "They still haven't confirmed they'll give full back pay, which is a whole other legislative fight, I'm afraid. But I have brought you two your money from the last two weeks of work, for what it's worth." He was a young man with sad eyes, red cheeks, and a bright blond goatee. He smiled regretfully as he handed over some coins to each of them. "Some places in the city still try to only accept Confederate money. If they do that, insist and then report them. And take the rest of the day off, kids. You deserve it."

Magdalys and Mapper blinked at each other. It was only noon. They had the rest of the day to themselves! They were out the door before Franz could change his mind, fresh stego-poop still steaming in the far end of the enclosure.

CHAPTER TWENTY-ONE
NEW SIGHTS AND SOUNDS IN AN OLD CITY

"**LOOK,**" **MAPPER SAID** as they stepped out into the cobblestone streets of the French Quarter. "I know you, Magdalys. What's going on?" An aging stegosaurus lumbered past them, pots and pans clanking on either side with each thundering step. Three raptor riders zipped around it amidst growls and hoots — one snatched a society lady's purse as they went. "Come back!" the lady yelled. "Thief!"

"What's going on is I shovel poop from sunrise to sunset every day."

"That's not what I mean and you know it."

He was right: Something had felt like it was festering inside Magdalys since they'd gotten back to New Orleans, but she honestly couldn't put her finger on what it was, and being on stable detail just seemed like the simplest answer.

"You feel stuck," Mapper said.

"I *am* stuck," Magdalys pointed out. "We both are."

"Yeah, but you have a mission to accomplish. And you can't. And it's making you want to strangle someone all the time. And I'm almost always the nearest someone! And I don't want to get strangled!"

Up above, onlookers gazed down from balconies with elaborate plants bursting from wrought-iron banisters. A group of kids and microraptors ran along the far side of the street, cawing and laughing with each other. It had just rained — but then, it seemed like it had always just rained when Magdalys went outside — and the early afternoon sun sent dazzling images of the city reflecting from puddles in the bumpy, uneven sidewalk.

"It's so pretty and alive," Magdalys said, deliberately ignoring how right Mapper was. Even New York, which had way more people and dinos, didn't feel quite this vibrant somehow. Everyone there was in a hurry to get somewhere, even if it was just to the next corner to beg, and it seemed like there was always a clock ticking away the moments nearby. Here, folks just lounged around idly for days — whole lifetimes probably! — watching shadows grow long from porches and balconies, wandering the streets in a slow meander, riding along on dinos or the streetcar and taking in the many wild sights of the city.

"Don't change the subject on me, Mag-D!"

"Fine! I'm stuck! I want to strangle someone! Everyone, really! What am I supposed to do about it, Mapper?"

He flashed a winning grin and wiggled his eyebrows. "I'm so glad you asked!"

She sighed. "Here we go. You have a plan, don't you?"

"Actually, I do not."

Magdalys mock-gasped.

"I have a suggestion."

"Oh?"

He swept his hand across the dangling ferns and street buskers and fancy folks and dinos of the French Quarter. "That you come up with a plan! A plan to complete your mission! General Grant ordered you to put a squad together and that's exactly what you gotta do. Who cares what stinking Banks thinks?"

"Well —"

Mapper waved off the point she was obviously about to make. "We'll find a way around that. The point is, putting squads together is the thing in the world you're second best at doing. You brought us together in Dactyl Hill, didn't you?"

"Not exa —"

"Nonsense! We all headed south into the middle of war together! Why? Because we believe in you, Mags! And sure, we got split up and everything went wrong, but that doesn't change the fact that we believe in you. And if we do, others will too! You're a born leader, Mag-D. It's not just dinos that you have sway over, it's us two-legged mammal types too!"

"I mean . . ." She really didn't know what to say. She'd felt it, seen it inside herself, and seen it in the eyes of those around her. It wasn't just that she had powers. People really did look to her for answers. "I just . . ."

This made three times Mapper was right in barely five minutes! It would've been infuriating if it wasn't also kind of touching. And anyway, he was also right about it being time to get to work. She would just have to find a way to put a team together when she wasn't on poop duty. And what better time to start than when they'd just gotten the rest of the day off?

"Hear that?" Mapper yelled. "It's a parade!" The ferocious thump of drums and deep *oompa oompa* of a tuba reached them from somewhere not far away. "Let's go!"

They headed off through the streets, dodging between the legs of a medium-sized brachiosaurus that carried what looked like a small ramshackle house on its back and hurrying past a chanting procession of nuns on ankylosauruses.

"Over there!" Mapper said. He grabbed Magdalys's hand and led her toward a larger street as the music grew louder and crowds gathered around them.

"Whoa!" they both gasped again as they stepped onto the wide-open throughway and took in the marvelous sparkling waters of the Mississippi River that seemed to wink at them from beyond all the ruckus and revelry of the city streets. A marching band swung around the corner as the music crescendoed with wild horn blasts and drum explosions. Four tall black men, each blowing through puffed-out cheeks on a brass instrument, stepped in time with each other at the front of the line. Behind them two women riding duckbills clanged cymbals together. The tuba player came next, his instrument coiled around him like a giant boa constrictor with its gaping mouth bouncing up and down in time to the beat. Behind him, three kids rode atop a huge alligator, each one wailing on a tiny clarinet. Finally, a whole squad of drummers took up the rear, their furious pounds and smacks echoing across the whole avenue and out over the river.

Magdalys had never seen or heard anything like it in her life. There had been the procession for General Grant that they'd flown into when they first made it to New Orleans, but that had more pomp and circumstance and not nearly the fire that this one did. Her friend Hannibal had told her about these parades, but being here, feeling the excitement of the people around her, the way everyone started dancing on either side of the street like some wild spirit was sweeping through on the warm Louisiana breeze, the crash of those cymbals! Magdalys wanted to live in this tiny moment forever.

But Mapper was already squeezing her hand again and pulling her somewhere else as the last drummer marched past. "What is it?" she asked, halfway wishing she could just follow the parade wherever it went, halfway excited to see something else brand-new and amazing.

"Don't you smell it?"

Magdalys realized she'd been breathing through her mouth out of habit from so much poop shoveling. She took in a deep breath of muggy swamp air, body odor, something tangy like beer or possibly pee, and most importantly: coffee! Amazing fresh strong coffee! And something else too, something sweet and freshly baked. They ran across the street, almost getting trampled by a decadently adorned iguanodon in the process, and stood in front of a bustling marketplace under a striped awning.

"There!" Mapper said, diving into the crowd. Magdalys shook her head, heading in after him, but she had to smile. He was so excited about everything, and when was the last time they'd gotten to have actual fun without being shot at or attacked by dinos?

Even as she thought it, Mapper was turning back toward her, a deep frown creasing his face. "What is it?"

He clenched his teeth. "Whites . . ." He rubbed his face. Blinked. "Whites only."

Behind him, white people from beggars to debutantes sat at metal tables sipping coffee and munching on delicious-looking, sugar-covered treats served by waiters in green aprons.

Magdalys's fists clenched at her sides.

They had been having so much fun, and here . . . here was

a sharp reminder that this world wasn't made for them, didn't care about them, barely tolerated their existence, in fact.

The smell of all that yumminess was making her mouth water. "C'mon," she said, taking Mapper's hand. "Let's get out of here."

"Children," a voice as old as an oak tree sang out from the crowd. "Not so fast, my dears, mmm . . ."

CHAPTER TWENTY-TWO
OLD ROSE'S SWEET CHICORY COFFEE

MAGDALYS AND MAPPER looked up and then farther up and directly into the eyes of a very tall old lady with a crinkled, dark brown face, pearl earrings, and a brightly colored head tie wrapped around her hair. She smiled down at them, leaning over a small wooden stand. A sign above her read OLD ROSE'S DELICIOUS CHICORY COFFEE AND CALAS.

"You don't want to mess with those cheap imitations anyway." Old Rose chuckled, swatting a hand at the whites-only coffee shop. "This here is the real stuff, the good stuff, my dears. Calas!"

"Who-as?" Mapper said.

"Ah, you are . . ." She squinted, then raised an eyebrow.

"You are soldiers, eh? Ahaha . . . In that case you get our special soldier discount, mm? Try a cala. For free! For free!" She let out a soft chuckle.

"Oh, no, ma'am, we can pay," Magdalys insisted, her fingers finding the coins in her pocket. She didn't want to part with them so soon, but she was famished, and she and Mapper had agreed to go out and enjoy the city together. "We just got paid today for the first time, in fact!"

"Ahh, I know, my dears," Old Rose said. "They finally decided to pay you what you're really worth! Heehee! 'Bout time, you know? Every man kills and dies the same, no matter how much you pay him. Every girl too!" She looked sad for a moment, then shook it off. "Anyway! Calas and coffee! On the house!"

"But —" Magdalys started, but Old Rose cut her off with two sharp claps.

Nothing happened. The crowd bustled around them. Magdalys and Mapper glanced to either side.

Old Rose rolled her eyes, clapped again. "Minuette! S'il vous plaît!"

A skittering sound erupted behind the counter. Old Rose sighed, waving her hand in a get-on-with-it gesture. "I swear. You'd think she was born on the continent! She's never even been there. She's just a pup, you know!" She disappeared behind the counter and Magdalys heard the sound of pouring and the gentle clink of silverware. "There you go! Allez, mon ami."

A short, squat ceratops waddled out, balancing a tray ever

so carefully on her back. It was one of the ones without horns, and it looked a little vexed to have been disturbed from what must've been a very pleasurable nap. The tray had two steaming cups of black coffee on it and a small plate of doughy treats covered in sugar.

"Go on, young ones, try it! Mm!"

Magdalys and Mapper glanced at each other. They'd been eating hardtack and crummy army ration coffee for what seemed like forever. And even before that, orphanage food was . . . mediocre on a good day, and rarely that. This though: This was clearly something special.

Minuette eased into a squat, impressively only spilling a little of the coffee, and then went back to sleep.

Mapper blinked, licking his lips.

"You first," Magdalys said.

He picked up one of the treats — calas, she'd called them — and put the whole thing in his mouth. "Wowww . . ." he moaned between chews.

"Ayee! Hungry children!" Old Rose smirked. "Dip in the coffee next time!"

Magdalys picked one up. It was warm and immediately covered her fingers in powdery sugar. She lowered it into her coffee, then took a bite. Doughy fresh deliciousness filled not just her mouth, but her whole body. It was so sweet, with the perfect twinge of bitterness from that strong coffee! So fluffy and light she thought honey might spill into her mouth with each chew!

A noise came out of Magdalys that she didn't mean to make, something like a sigh or laughter maybe; all she knew was she wanted more of that feeling.

"Yes?" Old Rose asked innocently. "You like?"

"I have no words," Mapper said. "Only the intense desire for more!" He grabbed up a second one as Magdalys finished hers and snatched the last one.

"No words," she agreed. "But, Miss Rose, you have to let us pay! We can't —"

"Can't what? Can't take gifts from a poor old lady? Ha!" She put an elbow on the counter and leaned her head against it, chuckling. "You know I was the first person to sell coffee down here in the French Market? Saved my money, bought my freedom, opened up this stand. I own this, you know? This is mine."

"Amazing," Mapper said.

"That's right." She smacked the counter, clapped twice. "Minuette! Reviens, s'il vous plaît." The ceratops grunted, lumbered back to standing position. "Merci." She waddled back behind the stand. "I am a businesswoman, you know. Which means *I* get to decide who eats for free. And you both, you are the freedom fighters of today. The heroes of our nation. You have already given so much, my children, and will probably give so much more." She shook her head sadly.

Magdalys couldn't tell if the old woman could see into the future and past or was just being poetic. Didn't matter really: She was right.

"And you," Old Rose finished, eyeing them both, "you eat for free."

"Thank you," they said, munching down the last of their calas and finishing them off with sips of coffee.

Mapper nudged Magdalys as they placed the empty cups and saucers on the counter. "What?" she whispered.

"She probably knows everybody who's anybody around here, and everybody else too. Go on! Ask her."

"Oui?" Old Rose said sweetly.

"Ah . . ." Magdalys made a face. She didn't want to ask for any more favors after Old Rose had already been so kind to them, but Mapper was right: If they were going to start getting their crew together, they had to start right away. And this was the perfect opportunity. "Do you happen to know, ah . . . who is the greatest dinowarrior in all of Louisiana?"

Old Rose raised her eyebrows. "Oooh . . ." She swiveled her head back and forth a few times. "Hmmmm!"

Magdalys waited, trying not to be impatient or disappointed. This whole thing just seemed ridiculous somehow.

"There is one, but . . ." She scrunched her face into a disgusted sneer. "You know . . ."

"What?" Mapper asked.

All at once, Old Rose was gone. Magdalys and Mapper glanced around.

"Did she just — ?" Magdalys started, and then a very short woman, barely taller than them, came out from behind the counter: Old Rose.

"Whoa!" Mapper said. "How did you . . . ?"

"Huh?" She looked taken aback, and for a moment Magdalys was afraid they'd offended her somehow. But then the old coffee seller shook her head with a smile. "Ah, I forget sometimes! It is Bonfouca." She nodded back at the counter. A sleepy ceratopsian face, this one much bigger, peeked around the side. "Minuette's father. He likes it when I give him scritches behind the ears. Anyway, it's a dinowarrior you seek? Because the most renowned one in the area, he is . . . I wouldn't send you his way."

Magdalys's heart sank. "Drek?"

Old Rose nodded, crinkling up her face. "A terrible, terrible man."

"I know," Magdalys said. "I've tangled with him already. Out in the Atchafalaya."

"And you lived!" Old Rose's eyes went wide. She examined Magdalys a little more carefully.

"Barely." The terror of those dinosaurs thundering toward her flashed back, that sinking feeling that no matter what Magdalys did, she'd never be able to fend them all off. That Drek had out-wrangled her at every turn. She'd panicked. She'd panicked and it had almost cost her and her friends their lives.

"There has to be another super powerful dinowrangler in New Orleans!" Mapper insisted. "One who's not some racist Confederate creepo!"

"Oh, well, of course there is!" Old Rose said. "One far more powerful than Drek will ever be."

Magdalys blinked at her. "Wh-why didn't you say so before?"

Old Rose chuckled sadly. "He's not a warrior, my dear. Not at all. But his skills with the dinos are legendary."

"Well . . . where . . . where is he?" Mapper stammered.

Old Rose glanced up at the sun, bobbed her head around. "Ah, it's time for a change of scenery anyway, no? And he should be in the square still at this hour. Come on, kids. Let's take a ride on old Bonfouca here and see if we can't find you your man."

CHAPTER TWENTY-THREE
JACKSON SQUARE

BONFOUCA WAITED AS Mapper and Magdalys climbed up onto his saddle; then Old Rose placed little Minuette in a basket hanging by the stirrups and hoisted herself up. Finally, she heaved up the big wooden sign — which turned out to be all there really was to the coffee stand — and yelled, "En avant, Bonfouca!" and off they went, water vats and dishes clanking along on either side with each of the dino's lumbering strides.

The ride turned out to be a pretty short one. They put the French Market and river at their backs, crossed a throughway bustling with dinos pulling wagons and chariots, then rounded a corner into a wide-open sunlit plaza. In the center of a garden area, a statue of Andrew Jackson gazed epically out at some imminent attack astride an iguanodon. Beside him, a young boy looked defiant, fists clenched. Magdalys scowled at it. Amaya had told her about President Jackson and how he'd implemented the forced removal of entire nations of Native people, which had resulted in thousands and thousands of deaths.

"Commemorates the Battle of New Orleans," Old Rose said. "The British came at this city with everything they had, and they still couldn't conquer it."

At the far end of the plaza, an elegant cathedral seemed to preside over the whole world, its three white towers rising into the sky and then narrowing into pointed gray spires.

"This must be Jackson Square," Mapper said. "That's the Saint Louis Cathedral!"

Old Rose nodded, chuckling. "Very good, my dear."

"It's lovely," Magdalys said. Down on the promenade below, fortune-tellers chittered and cackled back and forth from their card- and crystal-adorned tables. An old woman in rags slinked along behind them, shaking her head and mumbling to herself as two Union soldiers looked on from their duckbill steeds.

"That'll be Lafarge there, I'd say." Rose nodded her head toward where a crowd gathered at the foot of the church.

A sudden flash of color swished up over the onlookers. Magdalys flinched — the last time she'd seen a rainbowed flock of pteros, it had been Elizabeth Crawbell's killer archaeopteryxes wreaking havoc through the skies over Chickamauga. This though, she quickly realized, was another thing entirely. The shapes moved as one just like Elizabeth's had, but there was a precision to them, a poetry even, that those bright-feathered battle lizards didn't bother with. These pteros were about the same size — a little smaller than a chicken — but they had no feathers at all. Their little gray bodies were striated with patterns of red, blue, and yellow. And while a dactyl's crest reached back in a narrow point from its skull, these creatures had tall, sail-like shapes bursting from the tops of their heads, like mini versions of the sails on spinosauruses.

"Tupuxuara," Magdalys said out loud, taking in the gorgeous display the pteros were putting on as they flapped out of their initial tight formation and filled the sky, then suddenly resolved into a shape.

"Gesundheit!" Mapper said.

"No, silly. That's what kind of ptero that is. Oooh!" It was a heart, she realized. They'd formed two mounds in the sky above Jackson Square and now were filling it out with a pointed tip at the bottom. The whole crowd gasped with approval and then broke out into wild applause.

Magdalys had never seen anything like it. Sending dinos or pteros into coordinated attack patterns was one thing, but this . . . this was something entirely different. It was beautiful!

Around her, people oohed and aahed, their eyes fixed to the fluttering shapes above. A little kid grabbed her mom's hand and pointed at one of the tupus fluttering in little loops at the tail end of the heart. Old men on a nearby park bench put down their newspapers and gazed skyward, nodding their gentle approval.

A guy with a clarinet played a sweet melody to go with the flapping wings.

For as long as Magdalys had known she could meld her mind with giant reptiles, she'd been sending them to kill and die. Sure, it had been to save her life, but . . . it had never occurred to her that they could bring people joy too — pure, unfiltered joy, not just the thrill of making it alive out of a shoot-out.

"Ridiculous old goat," Old Rose scoffed. "He's just trying to impress me again."

"Oh?" Magdalys said. The crowd made way for them as the tupus fluttered into another chaotic splash of color.

"Thought I recognized that tired old ceratops coming this way," a voice called from below. It belonged to a hunched-over white man in faded trousers and buckled-up shoes. He leaned on a wooden cane and wore a wry smile beneath the gray mustache on his weathered face.

"Thought I recognized that corny sky nonsense," Old Rose grumbled.

The man raised one dark, bushy eyebrow and tilted his head. "All for you, ma belle fleur."

"Bah!" She glanced at Magdalys and Mapper. "He's been thinking that little pun is cute for half a century now because my name is Rose." Then she yelled, "Save it for your pteros, Lafarge. I didn't come to reignite tired old flames, eh!"

"Yowza," Mapper exclaimed.

Magdalys elbowed him. One thing she'd learned about adults was that if you stay quiet, they forget you're there and reveal all kinds of stuff kids aren't supposed to know about in front of you.

Old Rose glanced up. "Ah, you are too kind."

Overhead, the tupus had arranged themselves into the shape of a coffee cup, complete with steam rising from it and a spoon alongside. "I have my moments," Lafarge allowed with a wink. The folks who'd been watching his pteroshow dropped some coins in the donation bucket and started to gather around where Minuette was already prancing back and forth with a tray of coffees and calas at Bonfouca's feet.

"Now's your chance," Old Rose said, nudging Magdalys. "Go talk to him. Now you, young man —"

"Mapper, ma'am. They call me Mapper."

"Mapper, very good. Help me with these orders, s'il vous plaît."

"Oui, oui!" Mapper yelped, leaping into action. "How may I help you today, good people of New Orleans? Coffee? Caloo?"

"Calas," Old Rose corrected.

"Calas? Bonjour? Oui, oui?"

Magdalys shook her head and climbed down Bonfouca's saddle, then made her way through the crowd toward the steps of the Saint Louis Cathedral, where Lafarge tossed bread crumbs to his crew of tupuxuaras. They squabbled and squawked at each other playfully around Magdalys's feet as she strode past. "Good afternoon, sir."

"Mm? What can I do for you, little soldier? No more tricks today, I'm afraid. The tupus are all tired out and ready for their siesta." He let out a soft, rattly chuckle and sighed.

"No, I was wondering if . . ." Her words trailed off. How to even broach the topic? *I want you to join my elite squad of dino-warriors* just didn't seem like something you could walk up and say to someone. Magdalys remembered how careful Old Rose had been to differentiate what Lafarge did from Drek. This man didn't consider himself a dinowarrior. Not yet anyway. She would have to work her way up to it. "How did you do that?"

"Training, mon ami. These little tupus have been with me for many, many years now. I trained them since they hatched. Tupus are some of the most traina — What?"

Magdalys hadn't realized she'd put on a face of undisguised skepticism. Too late to go back now. "Tell me the truth."

"My dear child, I have no idea what —"

"That wasn't training. No dinowrangler could —"

He stood, face darkened. "Are you saying I am a liar?"

She stared up at him, traced the lines leading away from his eyes, the crease of his brow.

"People come from all over the world to see my pteros. They always want to find out my secret. My trick! Well . . . hard work! That's my trick! Discipline! Eh?" He smiled so suddenly, it caught Magdalys off guard. "You think there are shortcuts in this life? You think I'm special?"

"I know you're special," Magdalys said. Now she was smiling too. "Just as special as I am."

He cocked an eyebrow. "What?"

"But I know there's still hard work to be done. There's still so much for me to learn."

Lafarge just stared at her.

"I want you to teach me, Monsieur Lafarge. Teach me to be a master of the dinoarts. Teach me to be even better at reaching into their minds and understanding their thoughts. Teach me to —"

"Silence!" Lafarge's face trembled ever so slightly as he squinted down at her. "Enough! You are speaking madness, child. I don't — Ah!" His eyes suddenly went wide. Around them, a single tupu surged into the air, then swirled in a perfect spiral to form a dizzying ring around where Magdalys and Lafarge stood. It zipped suddenly low and then loop-de-looped into the air and landed with perfect precision on Lafarge's shoulder. "Hyacinth!" he gasped. "H-how . . ."

Magdalys took a step closer to him, still smiling slightly. "You know how."

"I . . . I . . ."

"Stop lying, Monsieur Lafarge. Teach me."

He gaped down at her, and for a moment she thought he might strike out, or run away in terror. Instead, his tight face eased into that suddenly whimsical grin of his. He shook his head, dragged a hand across his eyes. "You came with Old Rose, yes?"

"Yes."

"Very well. Tell her to bring you to my grotto tonight at seven."

Magdalys's smile grew wider. She released the tupu into a wild scatter across the skies. Took a step backward toward the crowd. "Thank you, Monsieur Lafarge."

"And little soldier," he called as she turned away. "Tell Old Rose to bring coffee and calas when she comes. Otherwise the deal is off!"

CHAPTER TWENTY-FOUR
LAFARGE'S GROTTO

"**L**OOK, CHILDREN," OLD ROSE said, bringing Bonfouca to a halt outside a large metal gate near some train tracks and, beyond that, the Mississippi River. A few tired dinos lumbered along the dusty road that stretched into the distance in either direction, but that was it. "Lafarge is a strange one."

"So we gathered," Mapper said.

"I know you need his help, and I'll do what I can to help you get it, but don't get your hopes up, eh?" Old Rose had brought them over to her apartment on Ursulines Avenue in the French Quarter, not far from the barracks, and whipped up a delicious dinner of seafood gumbo while Magdalys and Mapper filled her in on their journey so far.

"Why not?" Magdalys asked. "What's his deal?"

Old Rose shook her head, scowled. "It's not my story to tell." The gas lanterns on either side of Lafarge's gate flickered a warm glow against her face, danced in her dark eyes. "But he is a good man. And I trust him." She rolled her eyes. "Even if sometimes I want to strangle him."

The gate creaked and swung slowly open. Bonfouca strutted through and it seemed like they'd stepped right back into the bayou. Tall oaks stretched their thick branches across the sky. Little dirt paths led off into the greenery, and more lanterns cast their gentle glow on palm fronds, white jasmine flowers, and bright pink explosions of bougainvillea.

"Wow," Mapper said, blinking at some microdactyls at play in a burbling, moss-covered fountain. "I didn't think . . . I didn't . . ."

"You didn't think a lowly street busker could live so lavishly?" Lafarge's gruff voice said from the far end of the garden.

"I was actually gonna say I didn't think you could have such a peaceful slice of paradise in such a wild city," Mapper said. "But whatever."

"Ah." Lafarge strode out of the underbrush and grinned roguishly. "Fair enough."

"I mean, since you brought it up though," Magdalys said, "how *does* a street busker live so lavishly?"

"Come inside," Lafarge said. "You can leave Bonfouca in the garden."

Lafarge led them through a door, past a small, dimly lit living room, and then out into a wide-open atrium area with dino enclosures on either side. The familiar smell of poop reared up to greet them like an excited puppy.

Old Rose groaned. "I don't know how you do it, Lafarge. I really don't."

"What? The smell? Ha! Who even notices it anymore?"

"We do," Magdalys, Mapper, and Old Rose all said at once.

"And we shovel it in the Union dinostables every day," Mapper added. "Poop still smells like poop."

"Eh." Lafarge shrugged. "Small price to pay to be surrounded by God's most magnificent creations, in my opinion."

He does have a point, Magdalys thought, but she still didn't think she'd ever get used to that stench.

"Now." He walked out into the middle of the dirt-covered open area and spun around, his gaze sharp on Magdalys. "Before we begin, let me say this: no."

Magdalys cocked her head. "No what?"

He narrowed his eyes. "Let me see: You and your friend here, you are soldiers, I see. The Louisiana 9th, I presume, as most of the Native Guard has been deployed to Tennessee, from what I understand. You're not from around here. Up north, by your accents. Probably New York or Boston. And you've been through plenty, hm? Anyone of your race has, to be sure, but to have made the journey down here, well, I'm sure you've seen some things. Still . . . your face isn't altogether devoid of innocence either, eh? You are, after all, just a child. Twelve, tops, no?"

She just blinked at him. Dinos began emerging out of the darkness. First she just heard their grunts and heavy breath, the rumble of their approach. Then a trike appeared, followed by several ankylosaurs, a small brachy, two giant tortoises.

"Still, you carry a certain air of authority about you, don't you?" Lafarge said. "You are on a mission, are you not? Something of great importance. You don't have the bearing of an average foot soldier. You approached me in the square — Old Rose brought you, in fact. Which means you sought me out. Went looking for a dinomaster of particular abilities. And when you saw what I am capable of, you came and asked if I would teach you."

"I —"

He silenced her with a raised hand. "I will teach you. What I am saying no to is your invitation to join in whatever madcap adventure you have cooking up in that brilliant little brain of yours."

Magdalys's head was still spinning from how much he'd been able to figure out about her just from a glance. "But —"

"Butts are for pooping from, my dear child."

Behind her, Mapper guffawed. "Gotta remember that one."

"We just —"

"Show me what you've got."

Magdalys gulped. She'd expected to have to demonstrate

her powers again, but this whole situation had thrown her off. And anyway . . . she wasn't totally sure what she'd got. The truth was, nothing had felt the same since Atchafalaya. She was glad she hadn't had the opportunity to need her skills, because now that she'd witnessed what Drek, and Elizabeth Crawbell before him, could do, they seemed utterly inadequate.

She closed her eyes. Tried to ignore the sound of her pulse pounding away in her ears. Reached. The dinos surrounding them in Lafarge's grotto had a different feel to them from the others she'd wrangled. Most of those had been wild or poorly trained, she now realized. These dinos felt sharper somehow, ready. An underlying gentleness radiated through them. The ferocity was there too, but checked, like they had their wildness in reserve and could tap into it at will instead of in sudden fits of wrath.

Wromp romp wra-wrom, grumbled a nearby stego.

You, she thought, and felt it snap to attention within her. *Let's walk in a circle. And, you* — she turned her mind toward one of the ankylosaurs as the stego fell into a march around the grotto — *come the other direction.* He did, immediately, and so she sent three tupus looping through the dark sky above.

"Ahem," Lafarge said. He'd walked closer without her even realizing it — alarming little guy — and now stood staring pointedly at the far end of the grotto, where the stego stood chomping on the drooping fronds of a banana tree.

"Oh man!" Magdalys pointed a sharp thought toward him and the stego snorted and fell back into his march.

"Eh, eh, eh," Lafarge tutted, looking up and shaking his head.

The tupus had landed on the outer wall and were squabbling at each other. *Fellas!* Magdalys thought, and they fluttered into action again.

At least the ankylosaur had stayed the course, but even as she turned to it, the creature slowed down and eased into a squat, preparing to release a small mountain of ankypoop.

Magdalys glared at Lafarge. "Are you doing that?"

He chuckled. "No, ma chérie. They are."

"But I —"

"You usually have complete control over them, eh? As many as you want?"

"Well, not complete, but . . ."

"And when was this — that you have been able to control so many at a time?"

Magdalys looked down. "In battle, sir." She wasn't sure why, but she felt like that was the wrong answer somehow. She wished she'd grown up in a world where a black girl could just make dinos do what she wanted for entertainment. But she didn't have that luxury. Her skills had saved her life, plain and simple. And she wouldn't be ashamed of it. She met his eyes again. "We were under attack. Another dinowrangler was sending wave after wave of dinos to kill us. I . . . I was just trying to help my brother."

Lafarge raised an eyebrow. "This wrangler you speak of. He had red hair?"

"Yes, sir. Earl Shamus Dawson —"

"Of course it would be Drek. That pathetic little twerp. He tried to recruit me too, you know. And when I refused, he challenged me to a dinoduel. I have no time for these silly shenanigans. I sent him running." He sighed, shook his head. Then chuckled. "Arabella here nearly had him for lunch, you know."

A raptor gave what almost sounded like a little cackle from the shadows where she lurked.

Lafarge's face turned sour again. "He's no slouch though. How did you get away?"

"I bested him," Magdalys said as plainly as she could. "I stopped every dino and ptero he sent."

He raised both eyebrows, nodded. "Tell me how you did it."

"I . . ." Magdalys let her voice trail off, closed her eyes. Gave herself a moment to remember. Those spinosaur roars and the Bog Marauders' gunshots echoed back to her, brought a surge of terror. And then something else: She remembered the fire of her own anger as it welled up within her, how simple it had all suddenly seemed, letting that fire explode outward along her thought lines to the attacking dinosaurs, fending them off one by one.

That power.

When she opened her eyes, all the dinos seemed to have taken one large step closer. They stood all around, blinking at her with wonder.

Lafarge looked very serious; sad, perhaps.

"Rage," Magdalys said. "My fear became rage. And then I could do anything."

He nodded. "Come back tomorrow. We have much work to do."

CHAPTER TWENTY-FIVE
BACK TO THE BARRACKS

"**THAT DUDE IS** *so* weird," Mapper said as Bonfouca carried them through the midnight streets of New Orleans.

Old Rose laughed. "He is indeed, young Mapper. He is indeed."

Tiny dinos scurried through puddles, tumbling and squeaking at each other, chasing rats and scrounging for scraps. It was a cloudy night, and the darkness seemed to consume everything. Dim gas lanterns glinted on each corner; shadows ruled the city.

Magdalys's mind moved a million miles an hour. What had it all meant? She'd never been able to talk to someone so deeply about her abilities. She'd never been able to make sense of them. It had all felt like trial and error, stumbling through the darkness. It must've been like that for most people who could do what she could. Connecting to dinos was just a magical power of old or whatever. Seemed like most people hid their skills, like Hannibal had. It was only now governments were starting to recognize the military potential of having a true dinowarrior on their side. And of course, the Confederates were ahead of the game on that.

"You've known him a long time?" Mapper asked.

"Oh, child . . . almost my whole life," Rose said. She sighed. "Nearly killed him a few times."

"Go on . . ."

But now Magdalys had a chance to learn, really learn, and understand the power she wielded. She felt woozy with the thought. Sure, asking him to teach her had just been a ruse at first, and she still planned to convince him to join her crew somehow, but . . . he had answers! He was a candle in the night. And if she started learning this young, who knew what she could do. . . .

"Ah, those were different times," Rose said. "We've seen so many times in this little city of ours, you know. Been a tumultuous start, you could say. But we're still here and we're not going anywhere. I don't have any plans to kill that old goat anytime soon, so hopefully you can learn a few things from him."

"Wait, did you guys fight on opposite sides of a war?" Magdalys asked, suddenly interested. There hadn't been a major war since the forties, when the US invaded Mexico and captured a huge chunk of their territory. But there were always small battles erupting here and there.

"Heh, no, dearie, there are other things besides war that make people want to strangle each other."

A moment passed, and the sound of Bonfouca's clomping feet and the rattle of Old Rose's cooking equipment filled the warm night air amidst Minuette's quiet snores.

"I don't mean, ah, *actually* strangle, you know," Rose said into the quietness. "I mean metaphorically, of course. Just, ah, to be clear."

"Sure you do," Mapper said.

It was very, very late by the time they made it back to the barracks, said goodbye to Old Rose, and crawled into the bed at the far end of the room next to each other. All the other beds were empty, and it only reminded Magdalys that her brother was once again off somewhere getting shot at. And so was everyone else she cared about.

A single candle on a table nearby lit a tiny halo against the darkness. Magdalys was about to blow it out when Mapper said, "Wait."

"What is it?"

He looked at the empty beds, then the floor.

"Mapper?"

"I just . . ." He shook his head. "I miss the others."

Magdalys's heart felt like a setting sun. She did too. She'd just managed to shove all that missing away somewhere. It wasn't that she didn't think about them — she did, every single day. It was more that the thoughts were a sad wail, and if she was going to live her life with any degree of composure at all, that wail had to get muted. So she did. The missing had its place — in the way back of her thoughts, and so the wail continued on and on, but it never got loud enough to take over.

She put her arm around Mapper. "I know." Seeing him sad about it made the wail get louder and louder though. It was like their two sadnesses had finally found each other and were now having a big old sad party, whether Magdalys and Mapper wanted them to or not. "I miss them too."

"Do you think they're —" He just shrugged away the rest of the sentence, and Magdalys was glad. It was a useless question, and they both knew it. They probably weren't okay, and that was that. It was a war, the whole world was a war, and all their friends were black and brown and so they were tattooed with targets no matter what they did, how nice they acted or how hard they fought for freedom.

"Can we . . ." Mapper's voice trailed off again.

"What?" Magdalys was almost crying. Almost.

"This is weird, maybe? But —"

"Say it."

"Can we pray for them?"

Magdalys checked her first response, which was to bust out laughing. It wasn't that what he said was funny, it just came out of nowhere and caught her totally off guard. The matrons at the orphanage made them pray, but Magdalys was pretty sure everyone just went through the motions without paying much attention to the words or meaning. It seemed like something they had to do along with their other chores.

Mapper looked at her with such wide, expectant eyes, she was glad she'd swallowed back the laugh. Instead she exhaled solemnly and nodded. "Who . . . who do you want to pray to?"

He shrugged. "I dunno. Doesn't matter really, I think?"

That seemed about right. God seemed to have a million names — who could keep track? And she wasn't even sure if she believed in any of them. But she believed in the world around them, the beauty of the sky above at daybreak, and the thrill of sailing through it on dactylback, and that was about as much proof of a supreme being as she needed. "Alright," she said. "Close your eyes."

She did too, and the echo of candlelight sent little color splotches dancing across the darkness.

"You start," Mapper whispered.

"Ah, okay. To the, um, universe, and whoever else is listening . . . To the great big world out there and if there's a God, then to God too: This is Magdalys Roca here with my friend Kyle Tanner, aka Mapper."

"Heh."

"And we want to first and foremost say thank you for letting us stay alive this long in this cruel and scary world.

Especially considering this is, like, probably the first time either of us has really prayed for a long . . . like, ever, really."

"True."

"But we both try our best to be good people and do what's right in the world. And yes, we've . . ." Magdalys stopped abruptly. This wasn't confessional. There was no priest there to absolve them. She wasn't even sure if anything they'd done was *wrong* really, considering they'd done it all to save their own lives. She shook her head. Thinking too much as always. "Anyway! We want to pray for our friends, who are scattered all over the place right now and we just hope they're okay."

"Like Two Step and Little Sabeen," Mapper chimed in, "who are stuck in Chattanooga and surrounded by Confederates."

"And Hannibal, Big John, and the rest of the Louisiana Native Guard who are with them," Magdalys added. "Also, Cymbeline Crunk, who's on the way with General Grant to help them. Probably there by now, we hope. Plus, my brother, Montez, back in the line of duty along with his crew from the Louisiana 9th: Tom Summers, Corporal Hands, Toussaint, Briggs, and Bijoux."

"And Amaya," Mapper added.

"And Amaya," Magdalys agreed. "Out in the desert somewhere tracking down her destiny."

"And Cymbeline's brother Halsey Crunk, back in New York. And all the cats from the Vigilance Committee and the

Bochinche, like David Ballantine and Louis Napoleon and Miss Bernice. Oh, and Miss Du Monde, wherever she is."

"And Redd," Magdalys said. "Keep Redd safe on the high seas or on some wild adventure probably, saving the world with his red raptor, Reba."

"All of our dino friends," Mapper said.

"And our ptero friends too," Magdalys said. "Grappler and Dizz and Beans and especially big ol' Stella."

A moment passed. Outside, the coos and caws of dinos simmered on through the night. Magdalys opened her eyes. "Did we forget anyone?"

"Probably," Mapper admitted, opening his. "Your family?"

"Man . . ." Magdalys rubbed her temples. "I barely remember my sisters. But yeah: Celia and Julissa. Keep them safe too, please. You?"

"Terr-Terr and Fat Edson back in the Claw. And Meeps and Bala, I guess." He nodded with finality. "Oh, and you!"

"I'm right here!" Magdalys laughed. "You know I'm okay!"

"Right, but I want you to stay that way."

"Deal. I pray you do too, please."

Mapper shrugged. "I try." He settled in to sleep and Magdalys leaned over and blew out the candle.

CHAPTER TWENTY-SIX
PEUXP DEUXTY, PART DEUX

THE NEXT DAY, morning sunlight poured into the stables and Magdalys and Mapper were back at it, shoveling mountains of poop into a wheelbarrow. They'd already let the dinos out into the run pen and were about halfway done when a furious bugle sounded outside the door. They glanced at each other.

"Ten-hut!" someone barked. "Make way for the major general!"

Magdalys caught her breath. Could it be that General Grant had already made it back? He'd have news about her friends — maybe had even brought them along! And he'd be able to let stinking Banks know that she really was to be put in charge of her own special unit.

But instead, the nasal, sniveling voice of General Banks reached them amidst the clomping of boots and shuffling of clothes: "Very good, yes, indeed, alright then."

Magdalys sighed. At least they'd get news about Montez and the others.

"Ah, my new recruits," General Banks said, appearing in the doorway with an uncharacteristic smile. Magdalys held off retorting that she was Grant's recruit, really, not his. What good would it do? "How goes the duty of poop?"

"Stinks," Mapper said. "Sir."

"Sounds about right. You'll be relieved to hear that we have chased off those rascally Confederates and scattered them back among the swamplands where they belong."

Magdalys was relieved, but that didn't sound reassuring, somehow. It had been a whole branch of the Confederate Army, not just a gathering of angry guerrillas. They would've overrun the city if she and the others hadn't given warning. And they would probably form back up as soon as they had a chance. "Was it a fierce battle?" she asked, not knowing how else to get more info out of him.

"Ha, battle," he scoffed. "We simply demonstrated at each flank and they scampered off with their proverbial tail between their proverbial legs, you know. These backwoods secessionists bark quite a bit, but there's not much bite in them when it comes down to it."

Unconvincing, Magdalys thought. Grant would've chased

them out into the bayou, cut them off, and then destroyed the entire army and been done with it.

"Why didn't you smash 'em?" Mapper asked.

"Next year," Banks said, scraping something off the stable wall with his fingernail and frowning at it. (*Poop*, Magdalys thought with some satisfaction. *Gotta be.*) "Next year, I'm sure you know, is an election year."

"So?" Mapper asked.

"So in an election year," he said very slowly, as if explaining to a child (which he was, but still . . . Magdalys groaned inside herself), "battles matter, you see. They matter quite a bit. Elections are won and lost on the battlefield. If we don't start making some progress in this ridiculous war, for example, General McClellan may well snatch the presidency from old Abe Lincoln, and then we'll have a peace deal within hours, and then who knows what will happen. So battles are won at the ballot box and elections won on the battlefield." He chuckled. The man made it all sound like some clever parlor game, not a struggle for the survival of the nation with millions of lives hanging in the balance.

"Yikes," Mapper said.

"Yikes, indeed. And so, you see, next year, we will launch the Red River Campaign, and we'll win too, I wager, smash those Confederates clean across the swamplands. And it'll all happen just in time for Lincoln to bring old Louisiana back into the Union and we'll hold elections for state office, which

I'll win of course, coming right off a majestic victory like that, and then I'll go ahead with the hard work of making this place federal territory once again for real." He smiled magnanimously, as if all thanks and praise were due.

So this was what they meant by *political generals*, Magdalys realized. She'd heard the term many times, read it in the scathing editorials in papers, but hadn't quite understood it until this moment. General Banks was a walking example of it. She was about to make a mental note never to trust him with anything of value, except she'd already inadvertently placed her very life in his hands, and what was more valuable than that? If General Banks saw fit to, he could send her marching directly into the maw of battle without even a sidearm in hand, and that was that. The worst part was, if he did do that, it would probably be to assure himself election somewhere. She sighed. Such was life in the United States Army.

"The good news," Banks said, pointedly ignoring her dramatic sigh, "is that I've brought you back a little gift."

"Mags!" Montez yelled, running in.

She jumped up, catching his hug right in her face, and embraced him. "You're okay!"

Briggs, Toussaint, Summers, and Bijoux (with Milo on his shoulder) came in behind him, quickly followed by Corporal Wolfgang Hands. They exchanged high fives and hugs with Magdalys and Mapper. "You guys made it!" Mapper yelled.

"Of course we made it!" Toussaint scoffed. "What'd you think — we were gonna let you guys rescue us just to get blown apart a week later by the same fools that couldn't take us out in the middle of nowhere? Nah, man. Not the plan."

"Fair enough," Mapper conceded.

"It's good to see you both," Summers said.

"Well met, young privates," Wolfgang said, nodding. "I see you've been . . . shoveling."

"It's the worst!" Mapper moaned.

"At least now we can all do it together and get it done faster," Bijoux said.

Breeka! Milo squawked.

Magdalys gaped at him. "Wait, you guys are on poop duty too?"

"The soldier's life," Montez sighed.

"But you're, like . . . you're all, like . . . war heroes and stuff!" Mapper said. "You guys are *legends!*"

"I mean, who you telling?" Toussaint said.

"But also, if we're legends, what are y'all?" Briggs insisted. "You rescued us, not the other way around."

Wolfgang stepped in front of the others. "None of that matters though, Magdalys. We'll do what we have to do. What I want to know is: What's the update on the documents we got from the Knights of the Golden Circle?"

Magdalys gulped. She'd been shoveling poop all day every day since they'd gotten to New Orleans, and once they'd finally had a day off, they'd spent it tracking down Lafarge. She and Mapper looked at each other, then back at Wolfgang.

He shook his head. "Guess we better finish up poop duty so we can get started, then, huh?"

CHAPTER TWENTY-SEVEN
SECRET DOCUMENTS

"MAGDALYS?"

A woman sat in one of the shadowy corners of the saloon they were in, tinkling away at a piano. It was a sweet, ragged ballad she played, now timid, now ferocious, as if the song was discovering itself as it unraveled, a brand-new music.

"Hm?" Each note seemed to dance around another, like the true melody hid in the negative space of what was being played, and that dancing, jubilant bass run beneath made the whole piece seem perfectly undecided somehow, the happiest and saddest song in the world.

"Mag-D!" Mapper's voice.

How did that woman know Magdalys's sadness so perfectly? How could it be spoken to by a machine made of wood and ivory? The notes twinkled like tiny candles reflected in dark water; they slipped in and out of dissonance and harmony, formed shapes and explosions in the smoky saloon air made from the sweet tension and release, from silence and the low-register rumble of those bass keys.

"Hello!" Magdalys finally looked up from the hypnotic pianist, back to the table, where the fellas from the Louisiana 9th pored over pages from the file of documents Milo had helped steal from the Knights of the Golden Circle.

"You with us, sis?" Montez asked.

"Yeah, just . . . never heard anything like that before."

Montez smiled. "Yeah, you get used to it down here cuz it's everywhere."

"We made it," Toussaint bragged. "Took that ol' classical stuff and breathed some life into it, ya know? Put some flesh on those raggedy bones, hey, hey."

"We here to solve this puzzle and stop these Knights," Wolfgang said, "or we here to teach a musical history lesson?"

Toussaint acknowledged the point with a nod and clapped twice. "Alright, alright! Let's do this!"

Everyone leaned over and stared at the reams of numbers and symbols in the dim saloon.

The pianist wrapped up her song, took a long swig of something brown in a glass, and then started in on another. Magdalys almost wished the beautiful music would stop so she could concentrate better, but more than that she wished it would never, ever stop, and just follow her everywhere she went to remind her that she would never be alone in her sadness.

"Uh . . ." Briggs said after a few moments. "I know I'm supposed to be the intelligence expert of the squad —"

"That's never been a thing," Toussaint said. "Not ever."

"Yeah, you can unburden yourself of that expectation, B," Summers added.

Briggs waved them off irritably. "Point is, I have no idea what's going on with these numbers, y'all."

"Well, that makes both of us," Toussaint admitted.

"M-m-maybe it's some k-kinda m-m-m-medical information?" Bijoux suggested. "Mea-mea-mea-measurements?"

"Right," Wolfgang said. "But these numbers seem too big to be measurements, even for a dino. And they seem to be in a sequence. Or they grow at least, right?"

It was true: The numbers formed two columns across each page. The rows were labeled with numbers, and each column had a sequence of three distinct numbers: 45 2 17.27 | 83 11 53.3. Magdalys looked at the next line down: 45 2 18.87 | 83 50 72.3. Something was growing . . . or . . .

"Is it movement?" she asked.

"Movement," Mapper said. "Oh my god!"

"What?" everyone said at once.

"WHY DIDN'T I SEE IT BEFORE?"

"Man, explain yourself," Wolfgang demanded.

"I FEEL SO RIDICULOUS!"

"WHAT IS IT?" everyone yelled.

"Spit it out, Maps!" Toussaint said.

"Latitude and longitude!" Mapper said. For a few seconds, everyone just stared at him.

"Whotitude and whichitdue?" Toussaint demanded.

"He's right!" Briggs declared.

"C'mon, man, you're just saying that to sound like you as smart as the kid," Montez snapped.

"No, I'm serious! This one time when we were stationed up at Vicksburg, I found out where the Pinkertons kept their documents and I, you know . . ."

"You stole them," Toussaint said.

"I *borrowed* them! And they were full of numbers like that! But on their charts the numbers had locations next to them, right? And these . . ."

"They have dates," Magdalys said, pointing at the numbers starting out each row. "See: oh-four-oh-seven-sixty-two. That's May seventh, eighteen sixty-two."

"She's r-r-r-right!" Bijoux said.

"But why would a dino expert need charts with different locations and dates?" she asked.

Everyone grumbled and grimaced and got back to staring at the numbers, but there was a new excitement in the air now that they'd figured something out. A man walked in with a saxophone, nodded at the pianist, and started blowing along with her, mimicking the melody and then slipping into a whole new improvised part while she played along beneath.

"It's mind-boggling," Wolfgang said. "Numbers aren't my strong point."

"I'm still mad I didn't realize what it was till now," Mapper said. "I gotta track down an atlas so we can chart some of these points."

Wolfgang patted him on the shoulder. "Stop beating yourself up, kiddo. We should all probably take a break and get some rest."

"Oh shoot!" Magdalys smacked her forehead. "I have training tonight! Gotta run!"

"Training?" Montez asked.

"Tell ya later!" Magdalys yelled, already hurrying out the door and into the warm New Orleans air.

CHAPTER TWENTY-EIGHT
THE GATHERING

"**F**IRST," **LAFARGE SAID,** walking a slow circle in the dusty grotto around Magdalys, "forget everything you know."

"Like, about dinos? Or like *everything*? Cuz . . ."

"About dinos! Everything you have read in books, heard on the street, etc. etc."

"Did you read Dr. Barlow Sloan's Dinoguide? Because I actually thi —"

"Garb*age*!" Lafarge snapped, stopping in his tracks. "Absolute unmitigated garb*age*. The man is a moron in the first degree and beyond any hope of redemption. He is a cad."

"Wow."

He smiled, fell back into his stride. "Any questions?"

"Well, I —"

"No? Good. As I said: Forget everything you know. Everything you thought you knew about dinos. Forget it all. It never existed because it's all lies, eh? Eh. Lies and garbage. The dinosaur, and of course, the pterosaur as well, yes" — a single brightly colored tupuxuara alighted on Lafarge's outstretched arm and squawked once — "I didn't forget you, Hyacinth, no." He turned to Magdalys. "Everybody wants to talk about flesh and blood, tooth and bone, eh? Your friend Dr. Sloan, for example, is only concerned with the physical facts of the dinosaur."

"He's not my —"

"The temperament, perhaps, too, eh? But he is trapped, as all scientists are, in the realm of facts, of knowledge. A simple realm, for simple people, really."

"Yeesh!"

Hyacinth squawked a chuckle.

"But the dinos and pteros, they are creatures of emotion. They *feel*, Magdalys. Their feelings power their temperaments, their physicality, their physiology. And when we connect to them, as only you and I and just a few others can do, it is our feelings that are reaching them. That's what they understand. *Not* our thoughts! *Not* our science or our knowledge, eh? It is what we feel, Magdalys. Because we, too, are creatures of feeling."

Magdalys snapped her fingers. "That's why . . . !" Her mind was reeling. She'd never thought of it that way before, but it made perfect sense somehow, like she'd known it all along. There were so many moments from the past few months that gave truth to what Lafarge said.

"Yes? You were saying?"

But the one that stood out the most was what had just happened. "Drek. He . . . I faced him again a day later, and I couldn't stop his dinos."

"Go on."

"Just before that, my brother had sniped a dactyl Drek rides called Sweet Virginia and —"

"Ah, the crimson dactyl has been felled," Lafarge marveled.

"— he thought I did it. He already wants me dead because he knows what I can do, but after that . . ." She shook her head. "It was a whole other level."

Lafarge nodded. "Rage."

"But!" Magdalys waved her hands, trying to find words for her thought. Lafarge still strolled in his infuriating circles around her, hands clasped behind his back, Hyacinth watching from his shoulder. "My rage . . . it was . . . is . . . about something bigger. It was about so much."

"Oh?"

She'd been enraged not just for herself, but for her brother, for Mapper and the whole scattered Dactyl Hill Squad, for the folks enslaved on those plantations they'd flown over, and the truth that there were so many more plantations just like that all over the South. That so much of the world seemed to see her and everyone she loved as barely human at all and worth only what they could pick in cotton. That a whole war had to be fought, countless lives lost, to prove otherwise — even, it seemed, to those fighting to end slavery. She scrunched up her face. None of that seemed like anything she could explain to Lafarge. "I thought it was bigger, my rage."

"You have a way to measure a man's rage? Hm?"

"No," she admitted, not liking any of this.

"But it worked the day before. And then suddenly he had the upper hand."

"What did you feel at the time of the second encounter?"

"Just . . ." Magdalys tried to find a better word, but none came: "Fear."

Lafarge just paced.

"But other times, I've felt fear and still been able to do it," Magdalys said. "Like back in Brooklyn, the first time I tried to connect with a couple of dinos, we were in a shoot-out at the penitentiary and I was terrified! But it worked then."

"I'm sure it did. Sometimes fear will be an engine, yes, as with rage. But it's one thing to not think you can do much of anything and reach for the impossible out of desperation. It's a whole other to think you can do everything and suddenly, in the worst possible moment, with Death itself approaching, realize you cannot. It wasn't just fear you felt out in the bayou though, was it?"

Magdalys closed her eyes. "Panic."

"Mm, exactly."

She heard a flapping sound, then a soft pressure on her shoulder let her know Hyacinth had landed there. The tupu made little coos, lifting one foot, then the other while Magdalys just stood there, trying not to cry. "Exactly *what*?" she said, exasperated.

"Fear and rage, these will not do, hm?" Lafarge stood directly in front of her, his eyes sharp. "They are explosive. Sometimes incredibly powerful, to be sure. They are, in moments, unstoppable even. As you have seen."

"But?"

"But this is not sustainable, hm? This is not a strategy, not a weapon even. It is a mining accident, a hurricane, a freak occurrence. It will not be there when you need it. Its use is to show you what you are capable of, what you must hone."

"But . . . how? What?"

"There is something else," Lafarge said, not unkindly. "Something deeper. There are forces more powerful than your rage, Magdalys."

"Like what? Tell me!"

He stared her down. Seemed to consider something, then shook his head. "You must practice, Magdalys."

She slumped. "Practice? *Practice?* You *just* got through telling me that all dinos respond to is emotion! That all they are is great big feeling lizards! And now!" Hyacinth fluttered around her head, squawking as she yelled. "And now! After all that! You just tell me to *practice*?"

"Mm." Lafarge nodded. "Yes. And look." A dozen tupuxuaras burst out into the sky above them. "You are enraged again, eh."

"Urg," she grumbled.

"But listen, I will tell you a secret, hm?"

"Your secrets are never as exciting as I hope they'll be."

Lafarge beamed. "Aha! You *are* learning after all!"

"Go on . . ."

"This . . ." He closed his eyes. "This is the hardest, most important thing you can learn as a master dinowrangler."

"Taking a nap?" Magdalys asked. "Cuz . . ."

Lafarge shook his head. "Always in such a hurry. Pay attention."

For a few moments, Magdalys stood still and let the warm southern breeze brush her face. Far away, some church bells clanged out the hour, and the smell of poop wafted through the air. Then she looked around with a start — the dinos had gathered again. They'd formed a circle around where she stood beside Lafarge in the grotto and were slowly closing in. Magdalys had never known dinos to be able to move so quietly. "It's just like you did that first night," she whispered.

Lafarge nodded, opened his eyes. The dinos were all around them. "Any wrangler can make a reptile do cute tricks," he said. "Or summon a few to be by his side, hm? But the Gathering, the Gathering is something very special indeed. Once you can do that, well . . . anything else is child's play, eh?"

"Teach me," Magdalys said. "I've called dinos to me before but —"

"Only when you were afraid for your life, or full of wrath."

She didn't say anything.

With a wave of his hand, Lafarge sent the dinos snorting and stomping back into the trees at the far edges of the grotto. "It's not enough. You are very powerful, Magdalys, but with that alone, you will be destroyed."

"I —"

"Now! You try." He nodded. "The Gathering."

She glanced at him warily, then sighed, closed her eyes, and reached out. They were all around her, and the gentle rumbling of their thoughts rose instantly within her, a curious, bouncing tide. It was too much — she couldn't connect to so many at once, couldn't even sort through the endless strands of murmurs and coos to find one to start with.

She shook her head, straining for clarity.

"Calm, Magdalys. Calm." Lafarge's voice was firm but kind. "Remember I said to forget everything you know, hm? Don't do it the old way, eh? Stop straining so hard."

"How then? If not —"

"Shh!" Lafarge snapped. "Concentrate. Remember what I told you. They don't care how hard you pull."

"What do they care about, then?"

"Concentrate, Magdalys."

She did. She concentrated until the burble of dinovoices within her rose to a fevered, muddled wave that seemed to wash over everything, even her own thoughts. And surely, that meant they had heard her, felt her, and gathered.

A tiny pinch on Magdalys's shoulder pulled her from the chaos of voices within. When she blinked her eyes open, she stood all alone; only Hyacinth the tupuxuara stared back at her with those wide yellow eyes. Even Lafarge had walked away and was sipping coffee at a table in the far corner.

Magdalys sighed. "Hey, girl."

Papeena! Hyacinth chirped.

"Much to do!" Lafarge called. "Better try again, eh!"

CHAPTER TWENTY-NINE
THE BEGINNING OF A REVELATION

MAGDALYS WALKED DOWN the cobblestone streets of the French Quarter with her mind reeling. Nothing made sense at all, but at the same time, everything seemed to make much more sense than it ever had. And that in itself made no sense!

She'd woken up early and headed directly to Lafarge's, and she'd spent most of the next three hours sending pteros in wild spirals through the open sky above the grotto. Twice, she'd caused crashes that injured one tupu and really pissed off another. She'd spent most of that time pretty pissed off herself, in fact, but at some point, the anger had subsided — totally without her permission. A giddy kind of exhaustion took over and forced out everything else, and it hardly made a difference anyway: No matter how Magdalys felt, Lafarge was just going to say "Again," or "One more time, but better," or "Yes, but this time don't mess it up," when she finished an exercise. Exhaustion became irritation, which became anger again, and that sank pretty quickly back into exhaustion.

Still, beneath it all, the underlying thought remained: There was a way to learn this art, to get better at it. It had all seemed so random before. And that was fun, in a way, exciting. But it was also terrifying, and Lafarge was absolutely right that it was no way to go into battle.

"Cold fire, Private Roca," he said, over and over and over. "Too hot. Too hot and you will burn to death!"

She only barely knew what he meant, and at the end of the day, all she'd manage to Gather were tupus. First just Hyacinth and then the whole squad of them. It was cute and all, but it wasn't nearly enough. Not for Magdalys, and certainly not for Lafarge. "I think they just like you," he'd said. "That doesn't count as Gathering, I'm afraid. Although it must be added: They don't like very many people, the tupus."

Wild how much being in battle had made her able to accomplish miracles, she marveled as she turned a corner onto Decatur Street and headed past Jackson Square. It must be kind of like the way adrenaline made people able to lift incredible weights and run otherwise impossible distances. But at what cost? If she could learn how to do all that without the thrill of imminent death running through her veins, well . . . she'd be unstoppable.

"How was class, young Magdalys?" Old Rose called out from on top of Bonfouca. "Come take a coffee and calas on your way, eh?"

Magdalys was anxious to get back and hear what the others had figured out about the documents, but she couldn't resist Old Rose's offer. She veered into the crowded French Market, beamed up at the elderly woman, and gratefully accepted the treats. "It went alright. Just . . . you know . . ." She shook her head. How to even explain?

"He is a tough old cookie, eh?"

"Yeah . . . and I have a lot to learn. I feel like I thought I knew so much but really, I knew nothing at all and now I'm just barely catching up."

"Look," Old Rose said, suddenly serious, "if Lafarge didn't believe in you — and I mean really believe, because he doesn't do anything halfway, trust me — then he wouldn't be working with you at all. As long as I've known him, he's always refused students, and many have tried, from generals to pirates to diplomats."

"Wow," Magdalys said. She hadn't considered any of that before.

"He still insisting he won't help you out in any other way?"

Magdalys shrugged. She hadn't brought it up again, although in the back of her mind she still planned to try. "I don't think he'll budge, but that won't stop me from bugging him."

Old Rose winked. "Attagirl."

Magdalys finished off the delicious coffee with a slurp, placed the dishes on Minuette, and shoved the last bit of cala into her mouth. "Mmfangks, Miss Mmrose!" she called, hurrying off.

"Hey, Private Roca!" the kid selling flowers yelled as she sped past.

"Hey, Jupiter!"

"Mind the brachy dung," an accordion player said.

"Thanks, Salim!"

"Come back and grab some food later, Magdalys!" Felipe Petit yelled from the doorway of the little bar they'd been in the night before. Magdalys could hear the soft strains of that mysterious piano player twinkling out from the darkness within.

"Thanks, Monsieur Felipe! I'll try!"

She had no idea when all these folks had gone from being random faces on the street to people who knew her name and looked out for her, but somehow it had happened, and it gave her a strange sense of safety to be so recognized, cared for, in such a wild and faraway city.

Someone played an achingly familiar melody on trumpet on a nearby balcony as she rounded the corner and hurried into the barracks.

"Magdalys!" Mapper called from the top of the stairwell she was huffing and puffing up. "You're back!"

"Yes!" she panted. "I! Am!"

He met her at the second-floor landing. "We figured

something out!" He hopped up and down from one foot to the other.

"What is it?" She followed him up the next flight.

"I'm not sure exactly!" That didn't seem to dim his excitement though. Whatever it was, it mattered. "You'll see! Come quickly!"

Magdalys didn't have much more quickly in her, but she made it to the top of the stairwell and stepped into their bunk room. "Oh man," she huffed, planting her hands on her knees and leaning forward to catch her breath. "You did it again."

Mapper had tacked the documents to every available wall space, bed edge, desktop, and even the floor. It reminded Magdalys of the night back in Brooklyn when she'd walked in on the whole Dactyl Hill Squad trying to make sense of the paperwork they'd nabbed from Harrison Weed's house. That time, they'd uncovered the international slave trade conspiracy of the Knights of the Golden Circle.

These documents seemed decidedly more cryptic though. Magdalys swallowed back a gulp of sadness. Two Step, Sabeen, and Amaya were so far away. Who knew when she'd see them again?

"It's mi-mi-mi!" Bijoux said from behind a stack of papers. Magdalys hadn't even noticed him there. "Migration patterns!"

"Dino migration patterns!" Mapper added. "Pteros too!"

"Of course!" Magdalys said. "That's why those latitudes and longitudes were moving along like that, right?"

"Exactly! It all started to make sense once we charted a few out in the atlas we sto — errrr, borrowed from Banks's office!"

"And each pa — each pa — each page," Bijoux said, "is a different dino!"

Breeka! Milo agreed from his shoulder.

"But . . . why would the Knights want dino migration charts?" Mapper asked.

"I don't know," Magdalys said, "but we have enough to bring it to General Banks now. Let's go!"

CHAPTER THIRTY
OFFICIAL KERFUFFLE

THE FEDERAL OFFICES of the Army of the Mississippi were in an elegant mansion across the street from the Ursuline Convent. A dozen microdactyls perched on the railing of a nearby balcony, awaiting whatever message had to be delivered to the soldiers in the field next.

Magdalys, Mapper, and Bijoux rushed inside, snapping quick salutes at the guards on duty, and then they hurried up the winding marble stairwell to where an ancient and unimpressed white woman sat behind a magnificent desk adorned with only a small placard, which read: MRS. DEMILLE. "May I help you?" she croaked.

Magdalys had no time for formalities. "We're here to see the major general," she said, sprinting past.

"Oh no you don't!" Mrs. Demille sprang into action,

executing an outrageous spin jump from behind the desk and landing in a squat in front of Magdalys.

"Whoa!" Mapper and Magdalys both yelled.

"State your business or face immediate execution!" Mrs. Demille yelled.

Magdalys stared at her, panting. "I said we're here to see the major general."

"Regarding *what*, young private?"

"Regarding a top secret matter," Magdalys said.

"A likely story!"

There was an uncomfortable pause during which the old woman and the young soldier stared at each other across the gaudy carpet (they were about the same height). Magdalys heard a shuffle and clank behind her. Mrs. Demille's eyes left Magdalys's and then widened. Magdalys knew her friend Mapper well enough to duck just as a vase of flowers sailed over her head and exploded on the desk.

"YOUNG MAN!" Mrs. Demille screeched, lunging into a perfectly executed front flip toward Mapper.

"Mags, run!" Mapper yelled.

Something streaked across the room as Magdalys headed for the tall wooden doors at the far end: Milo!

Mrs. Demille landed and sprang forward into a jump kick but stopped midair and came down with a yelp. "Is that a . . . GET THAT VILE MONSTER OUT OF HERE!!"

Milo scrambled up her gown.

"AIIIIIIEEEEEEE!!!"

"He's not a mo — a mo — a monster!" Bijoux insisted, running over to collect the microraptor. "He's my fr-fr-friend."

"Mags, go!" Mapper urged. He had another vase in his hand, poised to toss.

"But —"

"BEAST!" Mrs. Demille hollered. "Unseat yourself from me!" She scrambled to her desk, dodging Bijoux, and retrieved a pistol.

"Ma'am!" Bijoux yelled. "Don't!"

"MONSTER!" Mrs. Demille screamed.

KABANG!!

The crack was near-deafening, and it was immediately followed by the shattering of the vase Mapper had dropped when he leapt for cover. Both noises seemed to reverberate endlessly beneath the tall marble ceiling. Magdalys glanced from the potted plant she'd dived behind; Mapper and Bijoux peeked out from similar hiding places. Milo was still clutching Mrs. Demille's shoulder pads for dear life; Mrs. Demille teetered back and forth, waving the pistol.

The huge door swung open and Banks ran out, accompanied by a small cadre of officers. "What the devil is going on out here?"

The two guards from outside came sprinting up the stairs, muskets at the ready.

"These children, sir!" Mrs. Demille hollered. "They've brought a — a —"

"Private Roca! Private Tanner!" Banks barked. "Private Bijoux! What is the meaning of this wretched cacophony!"

"We're not the ones shooting," Mapper protested.

"Put down that sidearm this instant, Mrs. Demille," Banks said.

"Then get this filthy scaled rat off me!" she yelled, still waving the pistol.

"Major General Banks," a calm voice said from inside the office. "Please get your people under control. We have much to discuss."

Magdalys recognized that voice. "Lieutenant Colonel Parker?" she gasped, standing up.

"Magdalys Roca?" Ely Samuel Parker's light brown, smiling face appeared at the doorway of the office, eyebrows raised. Parker was among Grant's most trusted advisers, which made him one of the most important people in the US Army. He was from the Seneca Nation, an expert engineer, and he'd been there at the Saint Charles Hotel when Magdalys had been given her special assignment. "Outstanding! General Grant will be so pleased that I found you!"

"Excuse me?" Banks demanded. "Are you trying to say —"

"Come inside, dear girl. We have much to discuss and this'll save me the trouble of having to say it all twice."

"Lieutenant Colonel!" Banks gasped, still flabbergasted. "This meeting is highly classified!"

"I tried to tell you," Magdalys said, strolling past him and into the office. "Mapper, Bijoux, you coming?"

"Now just a minute!"

"Are they on the team?" Parker asked.

"Sir, yes sir!" Magdalys said, snapping a salute. "And we have some intel of our own we're working on to let you know about."

Parker saluted back. "Very good. Come on in, fellas."

"Will no one rid me of this featherless monstrosity?" Mrs. Demille said.

"I don't understand what's going on!" Banks moaned.

"Come on, M-M-Milo," Bijoux called with just a slight smirk.

Milo hopped off Mrs. Demille, squabbled a shrill *breeka!* at her and scurried over to Bijoux.

One of the soldiers approached her. "Please put the sidearm down, ma'am. Civilians aren't even supposed to be carrying weapons in official army headquarters."

Mrs. Demille scowled, still clutching her weapon. "Preposterous!"

"I WANT TO KNOW WHAT IS GOING ON IN THIS OFFICE!" Banks screamed.

"Well, perhaps you should pay better attention," Parker said. "Now if you would come inside, I have some classified intelligence to go over with these young folks, and I'd hate for you to be left out in the cold once again."

CHAPTER THIRTY-ONE
THANKS, BANKS!

"FASCINATING," LIEUTENANT COLONEL Parker said when they'd finished explaining everything. "Absolutely fascinating."

Mapper had run back to the bunk to retrieve the documents, and now they were scattered all over Banks's office. Banks himself was slouched in a chair in the corner, blinking rapidly and shaking his head like artillery shells were falling out of the sky around him.

Parker stood, strolled along the reams of parchment, examining the numbers. "Banks, old fellow, what have your men made of this, hm? I'm sure the good doctor Thibodoux had some thought, no?" A few moments of silence passed as Parker kept squinting at the various sheets, and Magdalys traded glances with Mapper. "Banks?" He finally glanced over to where the general sat staring off at nothing. "You did have your men look into this, did you not?"

"We didn't . . . we didn't show it to him yet," Magdalys admitted. "We were actually coming over to do that just now, sir."

"Well, why on earth not?" Parker asked, blinking at her.

"The intel wasn't ready yet," Mapper said. "And . . ."

"And what?"

"And the general didn't b-b-b-believe anything they told him, sir," Bijoux said.

"It's true, sir," Magdalys said. "I tried to tell him about the role General Grant gave me, but he said I was making it up, and since the letter got soaked while we were coming back from rescuing the Louisiana 9th in the swamplands, I didn't have any proof."

"General Banks, is this —"

"It's all t-t-t-true, sir. I was one of the men the kids rescued. We wouldn't be alive if it wasn't for Magdalys and Mapper!"

"General Banks." Parker shot a stern look across the room. "Why didn't you take the young lady at her word?"

"Because it's preposterous!" Banks exploded, standing and waving his hands around. "It makes no sense! She is a Negro *child*, Parker! Why —"

"Lieutenant Colonel Parker."

"I swear the world has turned upside down," Banks grumbled.

"Excuse me, General?"

Banks looked like he was trying to squeeze his face into the smallest, tightest shape possible. "Never mind! What . . . How would you like to . . . proceed? From here?"

"There's the spirit," Parker said dryly. "How I would like to proceed is for you to believe what Magdalys and her crew say, moving forward." They stared across the room at each other, then Parker smiled. "Now, let me get to the reason for my visit —"

"Are Two Step and Sabeen okay?" Magdalys blurted out. "Sorry! I know there's important news to discuss, I just —"

"Last I heard, they were," Parker said solemnly. "But Chattanooga is still besieged, and General Grant was only just beginning to formulate a counterattack strategy when he sent me down here."

Magdalys exhaled and gave Mapper's hand a squeeze. At least that was some good news amidst everything else.

"Now," Parker said, "with everyone's permission, I'd like to continue?" He raised his eyebrows and made eye contact with everyone in the room. Magdalys, Mapper, and Bijoux all nodded. Banks made a little *proceed* gesture with his hand and slumped back into the chair.

Parker smiled. "Thank you. Our intelligence assets on the Mexican border have sent an urgent message. The Imperial Army led by Emperor Maximilian has nearly completed their overthrow of the Juárez government. Juárez was democratically elected and, more importantly, an ally to the Union cause.

The last remains of his army are currently holed up in a mountainous area near the border town of Matamoros, in the state of Tamaulipas."

Tamaulipas! Magdalys and Mapper glanced at each other, eyes wide. When Amaya had snuck away to find her father, the only thing she left behind was a note with three words on it: *Tamaulipas* and *Esmeralda Crusher.* Neither made any sense to Magdalys or Mapper, but now . . .

"How come I was not informed of this?" Banks demanded imperiously.

"You just were," Parker said. "Now, Juárez's forces are the only thing standing between your relatively small and soon to be outnumbered army, General Banks, and several hundred fresh divisions of fully supported French shock troops. Troops who, I hasten to add, will jump at the opportunity, are in fact chomping at the bit for the opportunity to link up with their Confederate counterparts on this side of the border and begin a continent-wide advance that could well wipe out all of us."

"Sweet Mary," Banks whispered.

"But they're sure to begin with the most vulnerable outpost in the heart of the Confederacy," Parker went on pointedly, "which is why General Grant has requested, once again, that you endeavor to wipe out once and for all whatever gathering of Rebel soldiers may be menacing the outskirts of the city, General Banks. This is of the utmost importance and should've been accomplished months ago."

Magdalys would've smirked at Banks being taken to task if

the situation wasn't so dire, but as things stood, nothing much was funny anymore.

"Sir, yes sir," Banks said glumly.

"Because now we have a near impossible situation on our hands," Parker said. "And with General Grant and Sherman's troops currently indisposed up in Chattanooga, as you know, we don't have the resources to fight a war on two fronts. Not to mention the president has given explicit orders not to get involved in any international kerfuffles."

"Might not General Trent be able to assist?" Banks suggested. "He's rumored to be somewhere out west, no?"

Magdalys looked at Mapper again. General Cuthbert Trent was Amaya's father.

"Rumored," Parker scoffed. "That's exactly the problem, isn't it? Old Cuthbert has cut loose, I'm afraid. We haven't heard from him in months, and the last messages we got were . . . unintelligible gibberish. Reports from the field suggest he's probably lost his mind, and he has some wild bit of machinery we don't totally know what to make of. But quite frankly, we have a war to fight and no one has time or resources to go chasing down every ridiculous madman who runs off."

Now it was Mapper who squeezed Magdalys's hand. He sent her a wide-eyed glance. She shook her head, squeezing back. That didn't sound good *at all*. But the worst part was, there was nothing they could do about it, and clearly Parker didn't know much more than what he'd already said. They just had to hope Amaya was okay, wherever she was.

"The real question is," Parker said, "what are the Knights of the Golden Circle planning? Magdalys, you said you overheard them discussing the Mexican situation when you captured those documents, correct?"

"Yes, sir. They said it was . . ." She tried to remember the exact words. "*This is how we win*, the one they called the Grandmaster said. He told them it wouldn't be in Virginia or Chattanooga, that what they were about to do would trap the Union Army in their pincers and end the war for good."

"Well, that certainly tracks," Parker said.

"Then he instructed Drek to head along the Mississippi, cross the Gulf, and embed with some guerrillas."

"I knew it!" Parker snapped. "They're sending a dinomaster into the fray at the border. Which means whatever those papers say —"

"We're already on it!" Mapper announced, gathering the documents up. "We'll figure this out, Lieutenant Colonel! Promise!"

"You better," Parker said. "I've already secured passage across the Gulf for you and your squad, Magdalys. You leave tomorrow."

She gaped at him. "We leave . . . tomorrow?"

"For the borderlands, my dear. Top secret mission. That is, if you agree to accept it. General Grant certainly hopes you will."

Magdalys looked back and forth between Mapper's and Bijoux's excited expressions.

"Wait a minute!" Banks said, leaping to his feet. "She gets to *choose* whether or not to accept it? What is going on here?"

Parker directed a withering glare at the major general. "I really would've thought you'd put all the pieces together by now. Everything this young lady has told you is the truth, although I doubt she'll be telling you much more from here on out, given how you received her the first time. Now, we have some highly classified matters to discuss, which I'm afraid are beyond your clearance level."

"I —"

"And anyway, you have an imminent campaign to prepare for, do you not?"

"I —"

"Now." He turned to Bijoux as Magdalys just stared at him, wide-eyed. "I told your corporal about one of my favorite little dive bars in the French Quarter. I wonder if we might meet the others over there. We have much to discuss!"

"We have ju-just the place!" Bijoux said.

CHAPTER THIRTY-TWO
DECIPHER

THAT PIANO WAS at it again.

The boys from the 9th were crowded around the table at their favorite saloon, running numbers and locations with Lieutenant Colonel Parker, and so much was happening, so much! More than Magdalys could wrap her head around, really.

But the woman tinkering away on that old piano in the shadows seemed to know that, somehow. Instead of the galumphing, low-down juke joint stomp, she sent the notes toppling over each other in sizzling arpeggios that rose and fell like nebulous mountains or the building tops of a cityscape.

For this tiny moment, Magdalys felt strangely at peace. It didn't make any sense — she hadn't mastered wrangling multiple dinos at once, and she had no idea what terror awaited her at the borderlands or if she'd have any idea how to face it.

"That's a four!" someone yelled. "Carry the four!"

"It is not!"

"Is so. And that makes this seventeen, and so that puts us smack in the middle of . . . wait for it . . . Wisconsin!"

Everyone burst out laughing.

She had a team, once again, against all odds. She had a team of incredible, talented, brave soldiers who would follow her into the gaping maw of death if she asked them to. They'd all set to work as soon as she'd explained what task lay ahead, and they'd done it without a second thought or question. It was like they'd been waiting all this time for someone to come along and finally send them off on a terrific mission into the wilds, and for Magdalys to be their leader.

"Guys, guys, guys!" Montez said, still laughing and waving his hands around to get their attention. "Just let Mapper do this! It's literally his name!"

"I'm saying!" Mapper groaned.

Briggs jumped up. "But . . . But . . ."

"RECONNAISSANCE!!" everyone except Parker and Briggs himself yelled together.

"You guys are no fun!" Briggs complained.

Parker shook his head. "Someone's going to have to fill me in."

"You're quite frankly better off not knowing," Wolfgang advised. "Trust me."

Mapper leaned over the table, squinting with concentration. "Okay, okay, okay! Let me focus, guys!"

"Fat chance of that," Toussaint scoffed. "But nice try, little map dude."

Parker stood, rolled his eyes, and made his way over to where Magdalys sat watching them all. "Quite a rowdy crew you've assembled, Private Roca."

She laughed. "Ain't it?"

He plopped down next to her.

"If I may, sir . . ."

"Go on."

"Isn't this a bit . . . *not* private, as far as places to discuss classified information go?"

Mapper was now standing *on* the table, eyes closed, making small circles with his arms while the others cheered him on.

Parker chuckled. "Which of these old drunks do you think is going to tell our secret plans to the Confederates?"

The bar had pretty much cleared out, Magdalys noticed. All that remained were the pianist, Felipe Petit, who was tending bar, and three guys nursing drinks in the corners. "Any of 'em could, really." She hadn't forgotten what General Grant told her the day after Drek escaped into the back alleys of the wealthy, white Garden District: *When our boys got there for pursuit, nobody had seen anything. Perils of a Union-controlled city in Confederate territory.*

Parker's face got serious and he nodded. "You're right to worry. Lets me know we've picked the right person for the job. Salchiche!" he yelled suddenly. "Check in."

The man who'd been slouched over a table near the door

leapt to his feet, back straight, and nodded at Parker. His overcoat swayed just slightly in the breeze coming in from the street, and Magdalys caught the glint of a pistol handle tucked into his belt.

She blinked at Parker. "Those are your guys!"

He tilted his head, mouth curved into a half smile. "Tiko."

Another guy Magdalys had taken for some old drunk sprang to his feet, nodded, then sat back down.

"Fremet." The third rose, nodded, sat.

They were all definitely armed and definitely not even slightly drunk. They looked like killing a man would make no particular difference to their day one way or another.

"All good, Lieutenant Colonel?" Felipe Petit asked from behind the bar. "Care for a drink?"

Parker shook his head and waved him off. "All is well, Felipe."

"He's with us too?"

"Mm-hmm. And Anabelle over there." He arched an eyebrow toward the pianist. "One of our best spies, as a matter of fact."

"I've never heard music like that."

"Mm, she's good at that too. You know folks come to establishments like this to spill their guts. What better way to garner information from an angry city, hm?"

"That's why the guys brought us here in the first place to go over the documents!" Magdalys said. "They knew it was a safe zone for their secrets."

"As safe as one can get. But listen." He slid a little closer and his face seemed to grow long, tense. "There are some delicate matters you need to understand."

"Yes, sir?"

"Since the president doesn't want to be seen as interfering in a foreign country's affairs, you and your team will be . . ."

"We'll be on our own," Magdalys said. "I understand. No uniforms, no identification."

"And . . ."

"There will be no rescue operation."

Parker nodded gravely.

"What else?"

She didn't think Parker could look any more uncomfortable than he already did, but somehow he managed. "The state you'll be operating in —"

"Tamaulipas." Magdalys decided to keep why she knew that name so well to herself.

"Good. You learn fast and remember crucial data. Yes, Tamaulipas. Besides being the site of President Juárez's last stand, it's a hotbed of rebel activity among the Apache Nation."

Magdalys kept her face even. Amaya's mom was Apache, and from the sound of it, pretty involved with the resistance. She'd instructed Amaya to learn everything she could from her father, but Amaya had always felt like that had been part of a deeper, underlying plan somehow. They'd been separated suddenly, before she could ever get any real answers, and that's what she'd gone out west to figure out. And Tamaulipas must figure into all that somehow. . . . Maybe this was how.

"I'm not sure if you know this, but the United States is currently at war with the Apache Nation."

Magdalys nodded. Amaya had told her about it. The United States was at war with the Indigenous people who had been here before European settlers came with their slave ships and poisoned blankets. And it was a war of extermination. One Magdalys would have no part of. She tried — failed — to keep the tension she felt inside from spilling out into her face.

"I know," Parker said. "I can't talk about it all. Not here, not right now. All I know is: *This* is a war we have to win, the one you and I are soldiers in. That's what matters most of all. If we fail at this, nothing else will matter anyway."

Magdalys just stared at him.

"And as Ely Samuel Parker, rank and designation aside, I'm telling you, Magdalys Roca, human to human: Stay out of that mess. Do you understand? Don't fall in with one side or another, because either one will spell certain doom. Don't get caught up in a whole other struggle when you already have one on the verge of collapse."

She kept staring. There were no answers in his eyes; she wouldn't let any show in hers. And she didn't have any answers anyway — the world was just a terrible place and that was that.

"I got it!" Mapper yelled amidst yelps and hurrahs. "I got it! Oh . . . my . . . god!"

"What is it?" Wolfgang asked. "What's wrong?"

Mapper just shook his head. "But what . . . does it mean . . . ?"

Parker stood. "Tell us, Mapper."

Magdalys shook off the strangeness of the conversation she'd just had, the creepy feeling it'd left on her. "Mapper, talk!" she called.

"Tyrannosauruses. Lots of them."

"I hate those things," Toussaint said. "What about them?"

"There's about to be about a thousand of them rumbling through the exact spot where President Juárez and his army are," Mapper said.

"But that's just a migratory pattern, right?" Briggs said. "That doesn't necessarily mean anything."

"What are the Knights p-p-planning?" Bijoux asked.

"A thunder run," a gruff voice said from the doorway.

Magdalys stood. "Monsieur Lafarge!"

Late afternoon sunlight poured from behind the old man, casting his shadow long across the saloon floor. He seemed to be standing up straighter than usual. Both hands gripped the cane in front of him in a way that somehow made it seem more like a broadsword than anything he'd need to help him walk.

"What's a thunder run?" Parker said. "And who are you?"

"He's my —"

"I am Lafarge," Lafarge said dramatically.

"Yes, I gathered that," Parker huffed.

"A veteran of the United States Army, and that's all you need to know."

"He's a hero," Toussaint said.

"He's my teacher," Magdalys finally blurted out. "And I was hoping he'd join our team."

"That I will not do," Lafarge said, taking a few steps toward them. "But I will tell you exactly what they're planning."

"A thunder run," Parker said. "You mentioned that. What is it?"

"Something that can only be accomplished by a master dinowrangler, I'm afraid. Earl Shamus Dawson Drek may be one of the only people on earth capable of such a feat."

"What —"

"It's a forced dinostampede," Lafarge snapped. "A virtually unstoppable assault. With a thousand tyrannosauruses, imagine a river as wide as the Mississippi but of only gigantic gnashing jaws and stomping claws, and then imagine it hurtling forward at fifty miles an hour in a frenzied race."

"It will utterly destroy Juárez's forces," Wolfgang said.

Lafarge nodded. "Indeed. It's not sustainable for very long, even for the strongest dinowrangler. But it won't take much to accomplish the destruction of an army. Just precision."

Mapper shook his head. "Wha . . ."

"That is all. I must go." Lafarge turned around and disappeared out the door.

Magdalys took off after him. "Lafarge! Wait!"

CHAPTER THIRTY-THREE
LAFARGE AT LARGE

THE STREETS OF the French Quarter teemed with life, as always.

Magdalys dodged a scramble of microraptors and wove in and out of bustling crowds. Up ahead, Lafarge moved with startling speed along the cobblestoned throughway and then dipped suddenly into an alley beneath dangling ferns and rusted ironwork.

"Monsieur Lafarge!" she yelled, shoving past a minitrike and clomping down the alley after him.

"Be gone, child. You have work to do! I can't help you anymore!"

"You lie!" Magdalys yelled.

The old man stopped. Water drip-dropped from the

balconies above, then plinked into dark, uneven puddles along the sidewalk. "I have never lied to you."

"We need your help," Magdalys said, pausing a few feet from him. Lafarge hadn't turned around, but she could tell from the way his shoulders rose and fell that he was breathing heavily. "You served once before. They called you a hero."

"I am a man of peace now," Lafarge said. "And that is that."

"Easy to say when your people aren't being enslaved," Magdalys muttered.

Lafarge finally turned, his old eyes catching her young ones, and for a few moments, the two just stared at each other across the alleyway. Maybe she'd pushed too hard, too soon. But the man was so stubborn! Like he enjoyed playing this whole enigmatic old guy routine. But so many lives were on the line. . . . Who had time for all that?

And anyway, it was true: Peace was always the easy route for those out of the line of fire. The pacifists up north wanted the war to end so they could go on profiting from slavery. But what was slavery if not a never-ending, one-sided war? Magdalys had had it with pacifists who would sit back and watch her die while feeling high and mighty about their moral choices.

She felt a presence growing around her a few seconds before she heard the shuffles and stomps of approaching dinos. Was this it? Lafarge could have her trampled or eaten in seconds if he felt like it.

But no. These dinos came gently forward; they pulsed with curiosity and something else, something deeper . . . compassion? The Gathering. Lafarge seemed to do it without even meaning to. What was the secret of this mysterious maneuver? A medium-sized trike emerged from the shadows near them, and then a whole family of raptors clacked gingerly up behind Lafarge, their heads bobbing and weaving, eyes glancing around. Three dactyls landed on the balconies up above, then four more. They squabbled and fussed at each other before falling into a subdued silence.

When Lafarge finally spoke, it was barely a whisper. "The British killed half my family. I was just a boy. Even younger than you are now, probably. I came home from hunting with my older brother, Michel, and . . . found them."

Somehow, the dinosaurs seemed to be getting closer to him without even moving. As more and more showed up, they filled the alley around Magdalys and Lafarge, grunting and huffing in the early evening air. The tupus from earlier flapped down from the shadows and landed on top of a stegosaurus, then settled in, looking on solemnly.

"I swore revenge. Swore I would do everything in my power to get it. And, as it turned out, everything in my power was quite a lot." He shook his head. "Quite a lot indeed. I had — have — this power inside of me. I didn't know what to call it, and at first I was terrified of it. Ashamed. But when we found my sister's and father's bodies trampled on the road leading to our house, well . . . I wasn't ashamed or terrified anymore. I just wanted blood to be spilled."

Magdalys gulped. Half of her wanted to run across the alleyway and hug him, for what he'd been through, for revealing himself to her. Half of her wanted to turn around and never come back. He had no right to compare his life to hers, even if he had suffered terrible tragedies.

"I joined up with General Jackson's troops. We were barracked just outside the city when word came that the British fleet was approaching. We were outnumbered and the fate of all the Americas seemed to rest on our shoulders. Of course, the war had already been won by that point, treaties signed. We just didn't get word until it was too late. . . ." He shook his head, scowled.

"I was just a drummer boy, you know. Just a child. I was a lot like you, in many ways. Wise beyond my years, but with a wisdom born from tragedy. Brave, probably too brave for my own good. Which is to say: reckless."

Magdalys swallowed a flinch. She had been reckless, if she was being honest with herself, but it still smarted to hear it from a stranger.

"I didn't have the guts to tell General Jackson about my skills." He scoffed a sigh, eyes gazing off at some faraway battlefield. "Wouldn't have even known how to explain it, not really. The British came with everything they had, but they were disorganized; they clamored against our entrenchments in pathetic, sloppy thrusts at first, and they paid the price in blood."

Magdalys took a step closer. "And then?"

"They kept coming." He spat the words out, horrified. "There were so many. They rode trikes and tyrannosauruses. A whole squad of ankys pelted us with buckshot. I just . . . I wish I didn't remember it, wish God had spared me these memories. If I could've just blacked out . . . anything. But no. It is all very clear, even now, almost fifty years later: I remember the terror and rage, but those are vague things, eh? It was the Gathering, you see, although I didn't know it at the time. The most powerful maneuver a dinowrangler can make. And I was the most powerful wrangler the world knew. But more than anything, I remember that tremble and click I felt when all those dinosteeds became mine. *Mine.* The queasy intoxication of it, the *taste* of all that power, of victory transforming in the space of one breath from something near impossible to a thing assured."

He locked eyes with her, and Magdalys felt nauseous herself, like some piece of all that heavy history had slipped loose from Lafarge and embedded itself in her gut. "Even today, even after everything that happened next, I still feel a sick sense of triumph when I remember that moment, that power." He flinched, disgusted.

"What did happen next?" she asked, when it seemed like he might have finished talking for the night.

"Come." He tipped his head toward the far end of the alley,

and Magdalys fell into stride beside him as they made their way between the serene crowd of dinos. "You see?" They stepped out into Jackson Square — this city would probably always feel like some kind of fantastic labyrinth, no matter how many times Magdalys walked its streets. The sun had set not long ago and duckbill riders now loped around the edges of the plaza, illuminating the gas lanterns as the daylight faded into a velvety darkness around them. "We won the battle."

He pointed out to the center of the park area in front of them, where Andrew Jackson stared endlessly off into nowhere from his iguanodon steed. And beside him . . .

"That's you!" Magdalys gasped. "The boy in the statue." She walked quickly toward it, vaguely aware of the mass of dinos stomping languidly out of the alleyway behind them.

The boy's brow was creased, his mouth a tight frown, fists clenched. She'd thought it was just anger, defiance, when she'd first seen it, but now she realized he was concentrating. "You're the hero of the Battle of New Orleans."

Lafarge made a harrumphing noise behind her. "Some say that. The history books don't, because Jackson had to be known as the true hero. Presidential campaigns and legacies demanded it, you know. And fragile political egos. But this city loves a hometown hero, even if the rest of the country prefers to suffer from ritually enforced amnesia. Of course . . ."

He walked up beside her, gazing at the statue of the boy he once was.

"Something else," Magdalys said. "Something happened."

Lafarge nodded, his face a cemetery. "I had no idea what I was doing. The dinos had never felt a power like mine. No one knew it was possible. They ran . . ." He shook his head, frown so severe it seemed like it might fall off his face. "They ran wild. Stampeded through the countryside and bayous."

Magdalys waited.

"Two dozen were killed. Trampled to death, mostly. My . . . my family. The only family I had left after what the British did. Michel. Jean Louis. Celestine. Mama. Only little Bienvenue survived, and only because she'd been sent to Lafayette before the war. The rest? Murdered by the havoc I created."

She reached out, unsure if touching him would help or make everything fall apart. Her hand hung there in the air, trembling. "You didn't turn away from dinos entirely after that."

"Oh, I tried." He coughed a curt, joyless chuckle. "Believe me, I tried. But . . . somehow, I couldn't. They were, against all odds, the only thing that brought me joy. I can't explain it. Who can make sense of these things? The healing power of the very thing that caused our downfall. It is as infinitely confounding as God." He seemed to dismiss the whole matter with a shrug. "But fighting, I gave up forever. That was my one vow that day. I couldn't forsake dinos, because they were a part of me, and there is nothing more dangerous than denying the most powerful part of yourself. But I would — will — never use them to fight again."

Magdalys nodded sadly. She'd made a similar vow not long ago, but it hadn't taken long to break it. No vow changed the fact that this world didn't care about her life or her loved ones.

"But this I know," Lafarge said after a few deep breaths. "Your anger won't save you."

Magdalys tensed.

"It may have gotten you this far. It may have done so once or twice, yes. But in the end it will only consume you and everything you love. It is combustible, Magdalys. It will catch fire and explode. Especially when you're dealing with a herd of rampaging tyrannosauruses."

"You don't know anything about my rage," Magdalys said. "You don't know anything about my life. What I've been through. What I've seen. What I've done. You think because you're old and have had horrible things happen, you know everything. But you don't. You've forgotten what it means to care about something enough to fight for it. You've made yourself forget."

"I —"

"Don't compare your pain to mine, Monsieur Lafarge. You'll never understand it. So unless you have a better suggestion than 'don't get angry when people are trying to kill you,' get out of my way."

Magdalys let the competing waves of anger and sadness wash over her as she and Lafarge stared at each other. She had no idea what Lafarge would say to all that, but it didn't matter much at that moment. All she knew was that she was tired of people telling her how she was supposed to feel, how to live her impossible life.

His fists were clenched, his face squeezed tight. He looked like he might sob or take a swing at her. Or both. "What do you want me to do?"

"Teach me," Magdalys said. "Teach me the Gathering."

"I cannot."

"Why?"

The old man just shook his head and walked away.

Magdalys stood there for a long, long time as the dinos slunk slowly back into the night, until all that remained was the squad of tupus chattering on the iron fence around Jackson Square.

CHAPTER THIRTY-FOUR
GOODBYE, HELLO

DAY BEGAN BREAKING in warm grays and soft purples over the Mississippi as Magdalys walked up to the docks. She'd spent the night trying to figure out the Gathering, failing miserably, and had barely slept.

"Ahoy!" Mapper yelled from farther up the boardwalk. "We got your minidactyl message. How was practice?" Montez, Tom, and Wolfgang stood with him, going through their equipment. A few feet away, Briggs, Toussaint, and Bijoux looked out on the river alongside Lieutenant Colonel Parker and a few of his men. Everyone wore civilian getups: brown slacks and white shirts with jackets. No emblems or medals, no extra cartridge cases or utility belts, just regular everyday clothes. Magdalys almost didn't recognize them.

She shook her head. "I don't know if . . ." She shook her head. "I don't know what we're gonna do."

"Mags, I've seen you in action," Mapper said. "You can do anything."

She sniffled and rubbed her face. That was exactly what she was afraid of. What if she did get all the T. rexes moving to her will and then they burst out of control? What if they trampled all her friends and Montez and then she ended up an old bitter mess like Lafarge? "I don't know. . . . We need a backup plan, something."

"Mags . . . It's me, Mapper. When have you seen me go anywhere without a backup plan?"

"I mean —"

"Don't answer that! And anyway, we have the whole voyage across the Gulf to figure something out. It'll be great."

Montez squeezed her shoulder. "And if you can't figure out the dino angle, we'll just sort out Drek the old-fashioned way like I've been saying all along."

"Quite a motivational speech there, big bro."

"The barge is due any minute," Parker called. "Gear up and get ready to move."

Magdalys and the others joined him on the dock. Mist hung over the water like a sleepy ghost. Magdalys shivered.

"You ready for this, Roca?" Parker said.

She shook her head. "I don't know, sir."

"I wish I could say there was room for mistakes, but . . . that's not the case. I'm not even sure if Banks is planning to launch the campaign we've directed him to. He hasn't shown much sign of it so far. For what it's worth, I believe in you, and so does the general."

Magdalys took a deep breath. A dark shape appeared in the mist, moving quickly toward them.

"We couldn't use any regular US Navy vessels to get you folks across," Parker said. "So we had to rely on some less . . . er . . . conventional partners."

"LAND HO, MATEYS!!" a voice called out of the mist. It sounded . . . familiar, somehow.

Magdalys perked up.

The first thing she realized was that the vessel was even bigger than she'd thought. A wide solemn sauropod face emerged first, its long neck reaching up from dark river water. An elaborate ironclad ship's hull rose from the creature's enormous torso. Cannons poked from windows all around. Steam-powered paddle wheels splished along on either side and both masts and smokestacks stretched into the cloudy sky from its midsection. A figure had been carved into the wood at the frontmost part of the sauropod mount — a boy with a cutlass and wily smile. It looked exactly like —

"Redd?" Magdalys gasped.

Someone waved wildly from the crow's nest at the very top of the highest mast. "Yoo-hoo! Up here!"

"Redd!" Magdalys and Mapper yelled at the same time.

"You know him?" Parker and Montez both gaped at the same time.

"Hop on, friends!" Redd called. "We have quite a journey ahead!"

PART THREE

MEXICO

CHAPTER THIRTY-FIVE
ACROSS THE WIDE GULF

MAGDALYS WATCHED THE two sharp sail fins of ichthyosaurs cut the swirl of ocean water. She could feel them, their shrill calls back and forth, their shock at encountering a being who could understand them, who could persuade them. Their curiosity felt like a warm breeze; their nervousness tingled and shuddered through Magdalys.

Out, she thought, and the two fins swung in opposite directions away from the hull. She nodded, waited a beat, then thought, *Now back*. The ichthys kept going. *Back!* And then they slipped smoothly beneath the waves and were gone.

Magdalys put her head against the sauropod's smooth tree-trunk neck and growled. The ocean stretched out of sight all around them. It went down and down and down forever, and held the churn and swoosh of countless gigantic creatures in its berth. It seemed so much huger here, from the middle of it, than it ever had from the shore. Huge and impossible and overwhelming, just like the task that awaited Magdalys when they landed. She bonked her forehead against the sauropod neck and groaned.

"Hey," Redd said, walking up beside her. "What did Phoebe ever do to you?"

"Urg," Magdalys said.

"More importantly, what did your forehead ever do to you? Phoebe probably doesn't even realize you're there."

"Urga burga."

Redd perched on the edge of the deck, legs dangling off, and gazed out at the swirling sea. "I don't speak urga burga, but if you want to talk about anything, Mags, you know I'm here for you."

Seeing Redd again had been such an unexpected blast of sheer joy, Magdalys had managed to forget about what lay ahead and throw herself fully into the excitement of heading off to sea with her brother and some good friends, new and old. They'd played dominoes, and had a delicious fish sandwich lunch, and laughed as Reconnaissance Briggs tried to introduce himself as a master spy.

Then they'd traded stories about all that had gone down over the past few months. Redd had fallen in with David and Louis and the others at the Bochinche (he assured them everyone was okay), hanging out late into the night and then roaming the Brooklyn streets on his raptor, Reba, looking for trouble. They'd inspired him to dedicate himself even more to the cause of freedom. It sounded to Magdalys like Redd had gone through a similar wrestling match with his own conscience as she had — he didn't really support a lot of things the US had done, but he wanted to do whatever he could to crush slavery. Finally, he'd decided to offer his services as a buccaneer but not join up fully.

The government had sent him on several covert missions, mostly interfering with Confederate vessels trying to break the Union blockade of southern ports, and he'd worked his way gradually south and then west along the riverways before General Grant sent a message that someone was needed to secretly transport an undercover unit to Mexico.

"The last time we had a heart-to-heart," Magdalys said, putting her head on Redd's shoulder, "we were about to storm a prison and I was terrified, and you changed my whole life with a few words just by getting me to be confident in who I am and my powers."

"Bah!" Redd said, waving her off. He put his head down on top of hers. "It wasn't all that deep."

"Was too," Magdalys said. "Anyway, now we're about to head back into yet another battle, and I'm terrified again and uncertain of myself again, but I don't want to keep dumping on you every time I see you."

"Well, that's the great thing about saying the right thing the first time! I don't have to repeat myself, since you already know you have to be proud of who you are and all you can do."

Magdalys let out a chuckle. "You make it sound so simple."

"Oh, no, trust me, I know it ain't."

A few moments of just whispering wind and crashing waves passed. "Tell me something good about you, Redd."

"Oh, ha . . . I fell in love, I think."

"Oh?"

"Twice actually. With the same person. Ugh. It's a long story. She's a hundred miles away and who knows when anyone will see anyone again in these stormy days . . . years . . ."

"What's her name?"

"Matilde." He said it like a poem. "She has fiery eyes and amazing aim and rides a minitrike named Poseidon." He shook his head, then rubbed his face. "Had to head back to France though. She's the daughter of Haitian diplomats and they were in some heavy-duty negotiations in New York and live in Paris, so we had three weeks of adventures and fun and then she was just gone. . . ." He sighed. "And it's not like I'm easy to find these days. She only has my address in Brooklyn, so there might be a whole stack of letters waiting for me when I get back, if I ever do."

"Oh, man . . ."

"Then again, there might be nothing."

"Redd . . ." Magdalys put her hand on Redd's shoulder. "I'm sure she wrote."

"Yeah, well . . . maybe. She was pretty upset when I told her I was going to run missions for the army. Said if I got killed without her she'd have to go hunt down all the people who'd killed me and it would really be a nuisance."

Magdalys snickered. "I like her already."

"Heh, you think she was kidding? Now tell me what's wrong with you. Seriously."

Magdalys affected Lafarge's battered old voice and Cajun accent. *"Everything you know is trash."*

"Oh wow," Redd said. "You found a grumpy teacher."

"Did I ever. Told me anything I've managed to do with dinos while in battle or afraid for my life doesn't count."

"Well, I mean, that can't be —"

"No, he's right. I mean, I can still connect to them, and I'm starting to get the hang of a few at a time, but . . . basically I'm back to knowing nothing."

"Not nothing, Magdalys. Everything you've done leading up to this still matters. You still draw on it to get to where you're going."

"Yeah." She scowled. "Seems like wherever I'm going, it's just to die." She turned back to the water, closed her eyes.

Redd put his hand on her shoulder, whispered, "I believe in you, even if you don't." She waited for the sound of his boots to clomp away.

Magdalys reached out. The sea was mighty, full of life. It churned, like a living thing itself. She could feel the rasps and moans, the eerie high-pitched howls echoing back and forth beneath the waves and through her core.

Come, Magdalys thought. *Gather to me.*

The moans and howls rose and fell within her. She felt no click of connection, but maybe it wasn't about that. Maybe it was something else entirely.

Forget everything you know, Lafarge had insisted. But he hadn't really told her what to do next. And then he'd just closed up shop and walked away.

Papeena, a tiny hoot sounded above the rest.

Magdalys blinked her eyes open. A single tupu sat on the ship rail in front of her.

"Hyacinth," Magdalys sighed, slumping forward, almost entirely alone. "Hyacinth."

CHAPTER THIRTY-SIX
LAND HO!

MAGDALYS AWOKE IN darkness to the sound of shuffling feet and skittering dinos above. What was happening? She'd gone to bed a little after sunset, worn out from a frustrating night of dinowrangling with Lafarge and then a full day at sea. She had no idea how long she'd slept; a circular window showed only night sky and crashing black waves. She was alone in the cramped sleeping quarters. Each long, raspy breath of the huge sauropod they were on seemed to rumble through the whole rickety hull, sending gusts of air and creaks of wood whispering back and forth.

She sat up.

That meant that Redd had cut the engine off. It was the first time since they'd left New Orleans that those huge paddle wheels on either side weren't swooshing amidst the churn and chug of steam. The sauropod drifted along on her own, swishing those gigantic fins through the water occasionally. Magdalys reached out to her and got an almost eerily serene kind of mooing as the reply. The sauropod, at least, was content.

Magdalys slid off her bunk and pulled on her boots. She stumbled up the steep stairwell onto the deck, where a brittle ocean wind swept over her. No one was around. That couldn't be right. She'd just heard them. Magdalys turned and exhaled. Everyone stood at the front end, their backs to her. There was Montez, beside Mapper. Colonel Wolfgang Hands stood with his arms akimbo, Tom Summers and Bijoux on one side, Briggs and Toussaint on the other. Milo sat on Bijoux's shoulder. Dizz, Beans, and Grappler were perched on the railing, and Redd sat astride Reba.

If Redd was already mounted up, Magdalys realized, walking toward her friends, that must mean . . . "Land ho!" he called.

"Well, there it is, lads," Wolfgang said.

"Don't look like much, do it?" Toussaint said.

"It's still two hours before daybreak," Mapper said. "And the rendezvous point is out in the middle of nowhere for a reason."

"I guess," Toussaint said. "But I don't like it."

"You don't like anything," Briggs said. "It's your whole style."

"What are we looking at?" Magdalys asked, coming up beside her brother and gazing out over the water.

"There," Montez said, pointing off to the side a little, where a tiny light flickered against the darkness in the distance. "It's the signal fire."

"Gear up," Wolfgang said. "We don't know what we're gonna find when we reach the shore."

They glided gently toward the flame, guns loaded, cocked, and pointed over the water. Magdalys realized it was a bonfire. She could make out a few figures standing around it, and the towering forms of dinos in the darkness around them.

"These better be our contacts," Wolfgang said. "Or we're fried."

"Ain't no such thing as fried," Redd scoffed. "If they ain't them, we turn around and head back. Maybe take some of 'em out on the way if they try anything cute."

"¡Oye!" someone called from the ocean below. Everyone turned their guns toward the man's voice. "¡No me maten!"

"He said not to kill him," Montez said. "¿Quién eres?" he called.

The man had slipped up close to them on the back of an armored plesiosaur. He stood in its saddle and held on to the dino's long, slender neck with one hand, waved with the other.

"¡Soy Ernesto Gael Ocampo Monserrat del Ejército Nacional! ¡Bienvenidos a México!"

Everyone looked at Montez. "Uh, he says welcome to Mexico. I think he's one of the good guys."

"I don't even know what good guys means anymore," Magdalys muttered. She wished she'd paid more attention when Montez had tried to teach her Spanish a few years ago. It seemed like such a faraway language now, but it was part of her, one way or another. She'd learn one day.

"We the good guys," Redd said. "Which means we gotta watch each other's backs."

"Hit him with the passcode Parker gave us," Wolfgang instructed.

"¿Dónde está el cuerpo de John Brown?" Montez called.

There was a brief pause, and then, in struggling English, Ernesto Gael Ocampo Monserrat yelled, "A-moldering en su grave!"

Magdalys saw more plesiosaur necks rise from the water around them. The dinos had approached underwater because they were riderless. They were there to bring them to shore. She glanced at Wolfgang. "Do you want me to hop on Grappler and get a feel for what's out there?"

He shook his head. "There's no way to do that without making it look like we're planning an attack. Everyone's on edge right now, and we don't want to give them any more reason not to trust us. They had the code, so we don't have any move but to trust 'em. Plus, we outnumbered. Redd?"

"Yes, sir?"

"I want you to stay on board Phoebe here and drop an anchor somewhere. We'll send you a microdactyl when we're ready to go."

"Aye, aye, sir."

Magdalys wished he'd be with them, but she knew there was a good chance they'd have to make a hasty exit.

"Let's move out."

CHAPTER THIRTY-SEVEN
THE GRUMPY GENERAL ZALAKA

A **GROUP OF FIGURES** awaited them at the shore. Magdalys couldn't tell if the dinos were still there; the night seemed impossibly dark. Tall shapes loomed near the horizon, but she wasn't sure if they were trees, or sauropod necks, or something else entirely.

"¡Apúrense, apúrense!" someone called from the shore, and the figures began scurrying about, their weapons glinting with the light of the campfire.

"Uh . . . everything okay?" she asked.

Montez cocked his head. "I think so? Hard to tell."

The plesios slid forward on the surf and then, one by one, the Louisiana 9th hopped off and made their way to the shore.

The cold ocean water shocked its way through Magdalys's

system like a splash of lightning. She had a carbine holstered on her hip, a dagger in her boot, and a backpack full of supplies. She still felt wildly unprepared and vulnerable. They could be mowed down at any moment, she realized. And no one would ever know what had happened to them.

"So," a gruff voice said as they climbed out of the waves onto the beach, "this is the *help* that the generous General Grant has deemed us worthy of, eh?"

Magdalys blinked up at the tall, mustached man standing before them with his hands on his hips. On either side, bedraggled soldiers looked around warily, cradling their rifles.

She gathered herself and stepped forward. "I'm Private Magdalys Roca of the Louisiana 9th, a newly created special division of soldiers and dinowarriors. We've been sent to —"

"Dinowarriors!" the man spat. "We ask for help and these idiotas in Washington send a bunch of . . ." He paused, whatever word he was about to say dying on his lips as all seven members of the Louisiana 9th stepped up beside Magdalys, their expressions promising a bloody international conflict. ". . . a tiny battalion of soldiers and a child."

"Two children," Mapper amended helpfully.

"And who exactly," Wolfgang said, stepping past Magdalys and throwing some growl into his voice, "are you to condescend to a group of soldiers who have put everything, including their very lives and the country they fight for, at risk to help salvage your cause?"

For a moment, the two men glared at each other, their

faces just inches apart. *Anyone could fire a shot at any moment*, Magdalys thought, *and we'd all be toast.*

"General Manuel Vicente Zalaka," the man said finally, and then, with an exaggerated sneer and a curt bow: "A su servicio."

"Well," Wolfgang started.

"And our cause does not need *salvaging*, thank you very much, but how very typical of you to think you could ride in and save the day, mm?"

"We have intel for President Juárez," Magdalys said. "There's a plan to destroy your entire army."

"Oh?" Zalaka seethed. "Tell me something I don't know, child! We've been hiding in these mountains for over a year, trading potshots with the French Imperialistas and their false emperor, Maximilian. We defeated one of the greatest armies in the world at Puebla, and we're wanted in every French-controlled state of México. Of course there's a plan to destroy us!"

"No," Mapper said. "Like a real plan. One that will work."

"Did a white man with bright red hair pass through your camps?" Magdalys asked.

"¡El gringo colorado!" someone said.

Zalaka shot her a fierce glare. "What if he did?"

She stepped in front of Wolfgang, who still was staring bullets at Zalaka. "That man was Earl Shamus Dawson Drek, a Knight of the Golden Circle. He tried to join up with you guys, didn't he?"

"¡Claro que sí!" someone else yelled.

"¡El gringuito colorado!" another agreed.

"The Knights are trying to set up a slave state across all the Americas. An Imperial victory would allow them to sweep upward from here and crush our army between theirs and the Confederates. Drek is one of their first-rate dinomasters. He's going to reroute an entire cluster of migrating T. rexes to stampede through your forces and wipe you out!"

Zalaka was staring at her, looking like if he clenched his jaw any tighter it might shatter. "Ocampo."

"Mande, mi general."

"¿Qué pasó con este gringuito colorado, eh?"

"Se desapareció ayer, mi general."

"He said he disappeared yesterday," Mapper informed everyone. Everyone groaned.

"I know you don't like strangers coming in and telling you what to do," Magdalys said. "I wouldn't either. And there's a lot we don't know about your war. I get that. But we're both in the middle of wars right now, and it's about to become one big war. And when it does, it'll be one that we lose if we're caught off guard and don't join forces. We need to work together." She realized she was out of breath and didn't know why. "I can stop Drek. I might be the only person who can stop him." She almost believed it herself. Part of her did, maybe. But Lafarge's voice kept echoing through her, reminding her of all the things she didn't know.

"How?" Zalaka demanded.

"I can do what he does with dinos. And I can do it better."

"We already have dinowra —"

"I'm not talking about regular dinowrangling," she said firmly. "This is different. This is something you've never seen before."

He held his icy gaze on her, still sneering.

"We need," she said again, as if somehow he would agree just on the sheer force of her willpower, "to work together."

The small band of soldiers had gathered closer as she spoke, all of them staring with wide eyes at this young, hard-headed girl in their midst. Magdalys was pretty sure if anyone demanded she prove her prowess with dinowrangling, she would explode. It was a fair thing to ask; she'd just had it with showing off. She was tired and about to face imminent death again, and she could barely be bothered with yet another hot-headed general who wanted to stand in her way.

Ever so slightly, Zalaka's face slackened. Then he nodded. "Break camp and load their gear on the brachys, compadres," he barked, without taking his eyes off Magdalys. Then, quieter: "I do not fully understand or believe you. But I will take you to see the president."

CHAPTER THIRTY-EIGHT
DESERT SUNRISE

THE SKY GREW purple and then gray as this strange caravan of soldiers and pack dinos rumbled along a winding dusty path between looming mountains and rock formations. The Mexican soldiers rode scutosaurs, a thick-bodied, flat-snouted beast that stomped along evenly on four flabby legs, glancing around with beady eyes and an alarmingly small head for such a stocky frame. They didn't move very fast, but those fiercely armored flanks looked like they could take more than a few direct hits without much toll, and a head-on collision with such a beast would not go well for the other guy.

Magdalys and the rest of the 9th rode one of the four brachys that had been brought in the expectation of a much larger landing party.

Zalaka, who had found no end of things to complain about ("we *would* have had use for these other brachys, you know . . . *if!* your little president had decided we were worth more than a meager landing party!"), stood at the front of the saddle and delivered a brief, testy roundup of the upheaval in Mexico.

The Imperial Army had shown up at the tail end of a brutal civil war, in which President Juárez and his liberal forces had routed a coalition of conservatives and church supporters. The remnants of the coalition had regrouped in Europe and gone to Napoleon III for support, swearing they'd back any despot he wanted to put into place over Mexico. (Zalaka had scrunched up his face and spat something nasty over the side of the brachy at this point of the story.) Napoleon sent an Austrian duke, Maximilian, to run things, and the Imperials had marched on the city of Puebla.

But Juárez's army had been ready for them, and their scutosaur-mounted shock troops rammed the Imperials with a surprise full-frontal assault and smashed them away with one desperate charge. Zalaka seemed to come alive with the memories of that warm May afternoon. The world hadn't seen a major world power crushed like that since the Haitians had overrun the French and decimated the first Napoleon's army. Everyone would remember that day for ages to come, etc. etc.

"But?" Montez asked, breaking Zalaka from his excitable jibbering.

The general's face soured. "But they regrouped. Napoleon

sent more troops. They got better supplies. They marched on us again, and this time they shattered our front line of shock troops." He shook his head, scowling. "Puebla fell. We had to evacuate the capital. Juárez sent Porfirio Díaz to hold the south and marched with us up here to open a new front along the northern border. . . ." His voice trailed off.

"And?"

"Pues nada." Zalaka shrugged. "We have been here ever since."

Magdalys was pretty sure there was something the general wasn't saying. His back had gotten very straight, and he gazed off toward where the sun had just begun to peek over the mountaintops. "We will be triumphant," he said quietly. "It is God's will. And God has sent us our great presidente to assure us of victory."

Who was this legendary Juárez? And what was the general hiding?

"What is your strategy, General Zalaka?" Wolfgang asked.

The general raised his eyebrows. "¿Estrategy? Heh, Colonel Wolfgang, my friend, our estrategy is to win!"

"I feel like that ain't it," Mapper said, but his voice was clipped by the sudden hooting of brachys.

"Ah, we have arrived," Zalaka said with satisfaction. "Let's see what our honorable presidente decides to do with you, hm?"

The caravan wound downhill around a narrow path surrounded by boulders. They came out to an open area shielded by steep, dust-covered hills on all sides — a perfect little hideaway.

"You don't need help, huh?" Wolfgang shook his head. "No offense, General Zalaka, but that's not what it looks like to me."

Soldiers stood scattered around the valley below. Almost all of them were limping or missing arms and legs. Some had bandages wrapped around their heads. Their uniforms bore the bloodstains of more than a few epic, terrible clashes. Some scutosaurs lingered at the far edge of the campsite, along with a couple knuckleheads and a small squad of microdacts. The dinos looked about as worn and busted as the soldiers.

"How many you figure?" Briggs said, nudging Magdalys.

She shook her head. "Two hundred, two fifty tops?"

"It's just under three, but I can see why you think that."

"General Zalaka," Wolfgang said. "This isn't an army, it's an infirmary. These men are in no condition to fight."

"Half of them can barely stand up," Toussaint added.

The general whirled on them. "You Americans don't know what it means to fight against impossible odds and win. We did it once, we —"

"Excuse me?" Briggs said, standing to his full bulky six feet and looking extra mean. "I don't think I heard you over the sound of us overcoming slavery."

"Hey, hey, hey," Wolfgang said, getting between them.

"You don't know the meaning of —"

"General Zalaka." The voice was quiet, serene even. And it came from above them. "Why are you being rude to our guests?"

The general's eyes went wide. *Above them?* Everyone looked up. A few feet away a man in a suit sat astride a dactyl.

But it was the dactyl Magdalys was staring at.

"Beans?" Mapper said.

Zalaka rounded on him. "Don't you dare address nuestro presidente as anything other than —"

"He wasn't talking to your president," Montez snapped. "He was talking to his dactyl."

Presidente. Everything had happened so fast, Magdalys hadn't had time to take in the man riding Beans. He had dark brown skin, intense brown eyes, and a tightly pressed mouth that curved ever so slightly into a smile. His thin hair lay flat against his head, parted sharply to one side. The president of Mexico was a brown man. He was Indigenous. She remembered someone saying he was Zapotecan, but she hadn't known what that meant.

But . . . how? How could a country right next to the biggest slaver state in the world have a democratically elected brown-skinned man as its leader? While the US was fighting a war of extermination against Native people, Mexico had elected one president.

"General Zalaka!" President Juárez said again, his soft voice suddenly sharp as a gunshot. "You disgrace yourself with your rudeness. I have already been alerted to how you've treated these fine soldiers. I wonder, sometimes, how you would treat me if I wasn't your president, hm?"

"¡No, Señor Presidente!" Zalaka stood up straight and snapped a salute. "I would never . . ."

"I have been waiting for the arrival of these men, but especially this powerful young girl they travel with." Juárez looked directly at Magdalys, smiled. "You are the one named Magdalys Roca?"

He said her name slowly, but not because he was trying to pronounce it right like almost everyone else. He said it like it was a melody he wanted to hear each note of.

She nodded. "Yes, sir."

"I apologize for the behavior of my top general."

"How did you know they were coming, mi presidente?" Zalaka asked anxiously. "Did you foresee it? In a dream?"

The president of Mexico rolled his eyes. "I foresaw it in the words written in the message I received. Now help, please, make the others feel at home as much as possible in our humble campsite, General Zalaka. I would speak alone with the young Magdalys."

CHAPTER THIRTY-NINE
THE LAY OF THE LAND

THE SUN WAS still low in the sky when Magdalys and President Juárez took Beans as high as he could go over the ranging sierras and wide plains of Tamaulipas. It threw long shadows across fields of waving mesquite grass and cypress and palmetto forests.

Magdalys had a million questions, but she wasn't sure where to start, or even if she was supposed to speak first.

"It is a very sweet thing, to ride a pterodactyl," Juárez said.

Magdalys smiled. "It's one of the greatest joys I know."

"It is important . . . to find joy." He sighed. "Even in difficult times."

"I sent Beans to scope out the territory," Magdalys said. "How did you end up on him?"

Juárez let out a rumbling chuckle. "I was on my morning

walk, partway up one of the hills around our camp, and he landed right beside me. I reached out my hand and stroked the top of his head, just the way the pteros back home liked. They also love it when you give them scritches underneath the jaw, you know. And then he let me climb up! I was very surprised."

A wild idea occurred to Magdalys, but she didn't know how to even ask. "Are you . . . Can you . . ."

"Am I special like you, Magdalys?" He shook his head, still chuckling. "I only wish. No, the dinos don't care what I am thinking. But my parents had a number of them on the farm I grew up on, and I have always loved them deeply. They seem noble, to me. Nobler than us humans, somehow."

The president spoke slowly, like he was plucking every word from a magnificent garden in his mind. It was a wonder a man could be so calm amidst such dire circumstances. Magdalys thought it might be a frustrating quality in someone else, but somehow she sensed that this man was not in any kind of denial about what was going on around him. She still had a million questions, but according to Mapper, the T. rex attack wasn't due till sometime that night, and anyway, what was there to do with such a small, broken army? Whatever was going to happen next, it would fall to Magdalys and her powers to deal with it. She took a deep breath of fresh air. For the moment, she just wanted to enjoy the amazing view and good company.

"War," Juárez said after a few moments of silence, "more

than almost anything else, is a time that shows us things are not what they seem to be."

"Oh?"

"You, for instance." His calm voice wavered with a gentle chuckle. "Small in stature but very powerful, no?"

Magdalys wasn't used to having her powers understood before she'd proven them. "How do you know that?"

"I saw it in a dream," the president said. Then he laughed. "Ah, I'm just kidding. General Zalaka is a fool. Your Lieutenant Colonel Parker is a good friend of mine, a . . . what's the word in English? Pen pal, you could say. He sent me a message about you."

"Ohhh . . ." Parker's sources . . . She'd never thought it would be the actual head of state. But it made sense somehow, especially given what Juárez had just said. "I guess you catch a lot of people off guard too, huh?"

"What, because I'm just a poor Zapotecan from Oaxaca, eh?"

"No! I mean —"

But the president was still laughing.

"Okay," Magdalys admitted. "Yes, I was caught off guard too. I'm . . . I'm sorry!"

"No, no, no." Juárez chuckled. "You don't have to apologize for the terrible things that cruel men have taught you to believe. You just have to learn when the real world shows them to be lies, that's all. That's how I got here, you know. I never thought I could get a degree, let alone become a lawyer and then, one day, president. But over and over, the world proved me wrong.

I had to fight for every bit of it, and I did. And here I am: riding a pterodactyl over the borderlands with a brand-new friend from New York City who also happens to be the greatest dinowrangler of all time!" His laughter seemed like it rang out over the whole countryside beneath them.

"I don't . . . I mean!" Magdalys tried to figure out what to say and then just burst out laughing instead.

"Look." They swooped a slow circle around the rising and falling sierras, and the rugged campsite came into view below. "It's not much to look at, eh? My little army. We are few and wounded. Even our dinos are starving. Soon, we may have to eat them. Over that way" — he pointed across the cactus fields to where Magdalys could make out a long dark shape in the distance — "is the Imperial Army. They are about four thousand strong, well supplied and, with the exception of last May, almost entirely undefeated."

"Four thousand?" Magdalys gasped.

"Mm. Not to mention this imminent threat from the Confederate dinowrangler you have come to warn us about. It seems over, doesn't it?"

Magdalys gazed out at the vast enemy army. Juárez didn't sound defeated — far from it. "My friend Redd says ain't no such thing as fried."

"¿Qué?"

She grinned, shook her head. "Fried means defeated."

"Ah, yes. Because, as I said, in war, nothing is as it seems.

Four thousand is just a part of the Imperial Army, you see. The other half is —"

"Down south fighting General Porfirio Díaz?"

"Ahh, you've been paying attention. Very good. Yes, and he's been crushing them, from what I keep hearing. Meanwhile, out there beyond the thorn forest, a settlement of Lipan Apaches has been sending out small bands to harass any army that gets near them. Whether they are destroyed or decide to join forces with one side or another could determine the whole course of the war."

Amaya's people. Magdalys wondered if she was there maybe, or if she'd found her father and figured out her destiny. She hoped she'd see her friend again, one way or another.

"And our friend Lieutenant Colonel Parker has dispatched General Banks with an army to reinforce ours along the border. If they show up — and I realize, knowing what I know about this Banks, that that is a big *if* —"

Magdalys snorted.

"— then their very presence may well keep the Imperials at bay, or perhaps provide safe haven for my army should we need to flee."

"But if that T. rex stampede reaches us first . . ."

"There will be no escape from that," Juárez agreed. "My point though is that the battlefield is more dynamic than it seems. We must always look deeper. I believe we will overthrow the French. The man who today calls himself emperor will one day be at the mercy of the very people he subjugated. The hungry cowards across the ocean from us who dispatch entire armadas to claim ownership of the world will watch their very empires disintegrate before their eyes. It may be in one year or a hundred, but I know it will be so, not from dreams or mystical visions, but simply because I look, and then I look deeper, and then I see."

"Whoa . . ." Magdalys's mind reeled with images of sinking ships, cities on fire. . . . What did the president see that she couldn't?

"Speaking of seeing things," Juárez said. "Is that pillar of dust in the west not one that would be churned up by a stampeding herd of tyrannosauruses?"

Magdalys's heart sank. The dust rose in a tall spiral over the nearby mountains. "They weren't due to arrive until tonight!"

"And over there . . ." Juárez raised a spyglass. "The Imperials are making their move."

"What?"

He passed it to her. A regiment of soldiers had detached from the larger army and now moved quickly across the plains toward them.

"They're trying to keep us busy with battle so we won't be able to escape the stampede."

"But . . . then their own troops will be crushed too!"

"A small price to pay for the total annihilation of your enemy, no?"

Magdalys sent Beans into a sharp dive. "What do we do?"

"I must prepare my troops for battle. As for you, young Magdalys, now is the time for you to do what you and your team have come here to do."

She shuddered, the wind whipping through her. "Most of my men will help you fight. I only need a few for what I have to face."

The frantic cries of a lookout sounded through the valley. "¡Ya vienen! ¡Prepárense!"

"Very well," President Juárez said as they careened toward the camp. "We have work to do."

CHAPTER FORTY
BATTLE
PREPARATIONS

"**M**APPER!" MAGDALYS YELLED, sliding off Beans and breaking into a run through the camp as word spread about the attack. "Montez! Saddle up Grappler and Dizz. The stampede is heading our way!"

"Already?" Mapper leapt up from where he and the rest of the 9th sat cleaning their weapons. "But! But!"

Around them, the small army began coming to life. Urgency spread like a wave as Juárez marched in long strides across the campsite, yelling, "¡Prepárense, mi gente! ¡Ya vienen los imperialistas! ¡Ármanse!"

"What do you want us to do?" Wolfgang asked.

"The French are sending a detachment to attack the camp so we're caught up in battle when the T. rexes crash through,"

Magdalys explained. "You guys hold them off with the others."

He nodded. "On it. Bijoux! Briggs! Toussaint! Summers! Gear up, fellas! We heading to war with the French!"

"Finally!" Toussaint said.

"Sir, yes sir!" Summers and Bijoux hollered.

Breeka! Milo squawked.

"Help those men hauling the cannons to the top of that hill," Wolfgang ordered. "And see what else needs doing. Remember, we're not here on any official capacity, so . . ."

"Don't die," Toussaint finished.

Wolfgang sighed. "Basically."

Bijoux made a face. "That might b-b-b-be easier s-said than done."

"That's a direct order!" Wolfgang barked. "Don't you dare disobey me!"

"Sir, yes sir!" the whole Louisiana 9th said at once.

"¡Son casi trescientos soldados!" a soldier at the top of the hill called. "¡Montados en gallimimuses! ¡Y vienen rápidos!"

"He says there are about three hundred," Montez reported as he threw a saddle over Dizz and strapped it on. "They're mounted on galli — gallimim . . ."

"Gallimimuses," Magdalys said. "That's one of the —"

"That, and they're coming in fast."

"— fastest dinos ever," she finished. "So yeah."

"I wonder why so few," Wolfgang said. "The Imperial Army has to have more men than that at their disposal."

"They do," Magdalys said. "President Juárez told me they're at four thousand. But they know those soldiers aren't coming back. They don't need to defeat us, just keep us tangled up."

"How far out is the stampede?" Mapper asked.

Magdalys had been trying to figure that out based on the dust cloud, but it was impossible to tell. Drek must've gotten to them early and driven them into a rush, probably assuming Magdalys would show up to try and stop him. "They were still a ways out, from what I could see, but they gotta be moving faster than we knew they could."

"Can we try to just get the army moved out of the way?" said Montez. "Pull back to the American side of the border, maybe."

"It'll never work," Wolfgang said. "A group this size would be impossible to move fast enough to dodge a whole onslaught of T. rexes."

BABOOM!! One of the cannons overhead burst to life amidst wild cheering from the soldiers.

Magdalys gaped. "They're that close already?"

The sound of rifle fire erupted as another cannon kaboomed across the valley. Up above, the cheering turned suddenly to yells and clashing steel. *They're on us!* Magdalys realized. She knew gallimimuses were fast, but she didn't know they were *that* fast!

"Up the hill!" Wolfgang yelled as the rest of the army ran forward around them. "We gotta do what we can!"

Mapper looked at Magdalys with wide eyes. "What do we do?"

"Right now," she said, pulling out her carbine, "we fight. Won't be any point in stopping the stampede if there's no army to keep them from stampeding through."

CHAPTER FORTY-ONE
THE BATTLE OF THE SIERRA DE TAMAULIPAS

MAGDALYS CLUTCHED HER carbine and turned toward the sounds of fighting, then stopped in her tracks. Gallimimus-mounted soldiers were spreading along the tops of the hills around them. Those tall, two-legged dinos with scrawny front arms and skinny necks galloped with long strides as their riders took aim with bayoneted rifles.

Blam! A shot burst out and Magdalys saw one collapse and then tumble down the hillside, its rider rolling over and over in the dust. But there were so many more. The Mexican soldiers ran to either side, shooting and stabbing with everything they had.

Chaos erupted in the camp. Gunshots exploded all around — the Imperials were attacking from three different sides at once. Tiny bursts of dirt flung upward as the bullets peppered the ground. Magdalys, Mapper, and Montez dove for cover behind a barrel of dried meat, but the tall, gangly forms of gallimimuses already stomped along the hillside in front of them.

"We gotta —" Montez said, but a group of Mexican soldiers rushed in front of them before he could finish and more shooting started.

From nearby, Magdalys heard the sudden squeal of a wounded dactyl. "Dizz!" She crawled around the other side of the barrel where Dizz was sprawled in the dust, bleeding from one wing and mewling softly. Beans and Grappler had crouched low and were nuzzling him, trying to stay out of the line of fire. "Come on, old buddy," Magdalys said, trying to ignore the sudden eruption of Dizz's frenzied caws of pain inside her mind. "I know, I know, Dizz." She grabbed his shoulder and then Mapper was beside her, taking the dactyl's legs.

"Oh no!" Mapper panted. "Not Dizz!"

"Bring him over here," Montez called. "They chased off the guys who were coming for us."

People were yelling all around them now, and the sound of steel clanging with steel and bodies dropping rose amidst scattered gunfire.

Magdalys and Mapper hauled Dizz around the barrel, and Beans and Grappler ducked behind them. They wouldn't be safe for long. "What now?" Mapper asked.

BLAM! Ba-BLAM! Montez let off two shots, each followed by a nearby scream, and then crouched beside them.

"There," Magdalys said, pointing up a hill to where one of the scutosaurs had been abandoned and was turning in circles, growling. She reached out for it and immediately felt a rumbling *bobadoo bobadoo* inside herself. The scutosaur stopped, raised its tiny head, and looked directly at Magdalys.

Come on, big guy, she thought, and the beast lumbered toward her.

Up on the hill behind it, the Mexican army had launched an impressive counterattack. They'd already cut down a lot of Imperial riders and were chasing another group of them across the hilltops. Down in the camp, chaos still reigned as soldiers and dinos ran every which way, cutting each other down at random and trampling bodies.

Blam! BLAM BLAM! shrieked Montez's rifle. A gallimimus shrieked and Magdalys heard it collapse in the dirt as its rider yelled something rude in French.

The scutosaur made his way obediently to Magdalys and then sat on his haunches, staring at her expectantly.

"Help me," she said, grabbing Dizz by the shoulders. Mapper took the feet and together they lifted the flailing dactyl onto the scutosaur's saddle. "Strap him down."

It took some work, but Magdalys kept sending Dizz calming thoughts with her mind and finally they got him secured.

Blam blam blam! Dust flew up around them as bullets rained down from above.

Go! Magdalys commanded. *Get out of here! Head for the thorn forest. There are people on the other side. Stay with them.* The scutosaur blinked at her once, then galloped off with astonishing speed, Dizz squealing on his back.

How much time had passed? She had no idea. In battle, a few seconds could seem like an hour. The T. rexes could be bearing down on them at any moment, and then none of this would matter.

"Montez," she said, "you ride with Mapper. Take Beans. We gotta —"

"Watch out!" Montez yelled, and then Magdalys felt her whole body fly backward as a sharp blast of pain tore through her shoulder.

"Magdalys!" Mapper screamed.

She was on the ground, on her back, dust wafting up from where she'd fallen, bullets still singing past overhead. Was she dead?

Mapper and Montez crouched over her, their faces twisted with concern. "Are you okay?" Montez said, wiping his eyes. "Please be okay."

Her shoulder stung but she could move everything. "I think so?" She let them help her up, looked down. Blood soaked her sleeve, but she could feel the wound and it didn't seem too deep. Definitely nothing important had been hit.

BLAM BLAM BLAM! The Imperials were getting closer. Those tall beasts leapt forward in groups of two or three, and then sank into a crouch for just long enough to let the rider get off a few shots. Then they flitted back to the front lines like awkward ballerinas of death.

"Can you stand?" Mapper asked, offering his hand.

"Yeah." She took it, pulled herself to her feet but stayed at a low crouch behind the barrels. "But how are we gonna get out of here? We're hemmed in."

Montez glanced around, shook his head. "Just gotta make a run for it, I guess. The T. rexes'll be on us any minute."

Magdalys glanced at the sky, saw no pillars of dust in the distance, thankfully, but it was only a matter of time. "Ready?"

Montez and Mapper nodded, but they looked terrified.

"HEEEEYAH!!!" came a yell from nearby, and then the sound of thundering feet.

Magdalys whirled around. Was it the stampede already? Could they have snuck up on them like that? Instead, Magdalys almost leapt for joy as Colonel Wolfgang Hands came galloping toward them on scutoback along with Summers, Toussaint, Briggs, and Bijoux, two to a scutosaur. A whole crew of Mexican soldiers rode with them, firing off their rifles in every direction and whooping wildly.

"¡VIVA MÉXICO!" Briggs yelled in a terrible accent.

"You guys get out of here!" Wolfgang called, blasting away with a six-shooter. "We'll keep these fancy clowns busy!"

Magdalys almost burst into tears with relief. Instead she firmed her face, nodded sharply, and used her nonwounded arm to climb up on Grappler as the Mexican soldiers and Louisiana 9th charged the French lines, guns blazing.

The Imperial gallimimus riders danced back a few paces as if winding up and then burst forward with blades drawn, flooding through the scutosaur attack. Dust rose over the skirmish like a curtain from below, but Magdalys could make out the shapes of those tall, skinny dinos prancing through the rows of mounted riders. She saw two collapse beneath the fray, saw another Imperial slash a Mexican soldier and then leap over the tumbling catastrophe of his panicked scutosaur and keep fighting.

Montez started to climb up behind her but she stopped him. "You ride with Mapper," she said.

"But your arm, Mags!"

She shook her head. "I'm alright." It was mostly true. Sure, she'd just been shot, but it hadn't gone deep. And anyway, this was no time to get sentimental. "Ride with Mapper. Find Drek and take him out. He'll be hiding, but he's got to keep moving somehow to keep up with the herd. The second he surfaces, take the shot. And don't . . . !"

Montez was already giving her a know-it-all face.

Magdalys sighed. "Yes, Montez Gabriel Roca, you were right . . ."

"Thank you."

". . . from a certain point of view."

He rolled his eyes. "Ugh! Who says that? You're impossible."

"The wrong point of view, just to clarify."

"If you'da let me —"

"I know, I know," Magdalys said, spurring Grappler into the air. "You'll get your toldya so when all this is over! Just take the shot if you got it!" She flew up over the fighting and then zoomed off toward where the billowing cloud of dust raced their way.

CHAPTER FORTY-TWO
THUNDER RUN

DESERT MOUNTAINS SLID past beneath Magdalys. Off to her right, the thorn forest sprawled along the hillsides; somewhere beyond that was the Apache encampment. To her left, the foothills gave way to a wide-open, shrub-covered plain, the Imperial Army a muddled collection of splotches near the horizon.

The bright sun glared angrily from directly above, splashed a rippling shadow of Grappler's spread wings over the sierras below.

And up ahead: the dust cloud.

Magdalys could already hear the rumble of all those T. rex feet stomping along toward her.

Mapper and Montez would be flying not far behind, probably sweeping wide swaths over the countryside to find Drek.

And maybe they would, and all this would be over long enough for everyone to catch their breath and regroup.

But even then: The Imperial Army was ten times their size. Banks might never show up. . . . A million things could go wrong, and it seemed like utter annihilation waited one wrong move away. Even if they did everything right, whatever that meant, they could all be wiped out as a slaver empire swept the continent.

She shook her head, taking Grappler low and then banking left around a mountaintop.

This whole ugly world was an impossible puzzle, and they hadn't even given her all the pieces.

Anger burned through her, as familiar as an old friend.

Sure, Lafarge had warned her against it, but what else did she have? What was she supposed to tap into if not that? Or should she just allow these demon fools to rule the world and destroy her loved ones?

No.

That wasn't the way.

She breathed deep and allowed those fires to grow within her, felt Grappler burst forward with a new blast of energy, fueled by the same wrath as Magdalys was.

"Come on, girl." Magdalys's voice was a hoarse whisper. "These creeps hurt you, hurt Dizz, and they're trying to run us into the sea. Let's end this."

They swooped over a wide plateau and then suddenly swung hard to the right. That mountain of dust was closer than she'd realized. Down below, the whole planet seemed to seethe and shake as hundreds of T. rexes trundled along through the valley, all growls, roars, and stomps. Most of them were grayish or tan-colored with brown-and-purple stripes along their backs. They had flimsy feathers along their limbs and throats, and they were moving faster than Magdalys had ever imagined a T. rex should be able to move.

Magdalys was about to take Grappler into a dive when *BLAM!!* a bullet whizzed past from out of nowhere.

She veered left and then pulled hard on the reins, sending Grappler up over the dust cloud. Below her, one dactylrider, then another emerged from the swirl and swooped around toward her.

They were both dressed in white robes with white hoods, and they rode albino dactyls — all white with pale pink eyes. Could one of them be Drek? Magdalys flushed out over the sky, pulling out her carbine and prepping it.

BLAM BLAM! Two more shots sizzled past, just over her head. These guys weren't average soldiers; if she'd been sitting up straight, one of those might've brained her, and that would've been that. The Sky Raiders! She'd overhead that old man mention them when she was hiding in the chimney back in the Atchafalaya hideaway! He'd said two Sky Raiders would accompany Drek on his mission.

She dropped Grappler low and then swung her around, ready to let off a shot as she spun to face them. Instead, a rifle blast rang out from somewhere nearby and one of the men shrieked and flung forward off his mount, hurtling toward the racing T. rexes below. The other Raider went into a sharp dive.

Magdalys looked up, heart thundering.

"Heyoo!" Mapper yelled, sending Beans down after the Raider. Behind him, Montez held his rifle up and readied another shot.

"Thanks, boys!" Magdalys called, and then spun Grappler low and away from the others. She had to get these T. rexes under her control now or it wouldn't matter how many Sky Raiders they took out.

The rumble and growls grew louder as they glided just above those gnashing teeth.

"Right there," Magdalys said, eyeing a tall, gray tyrannosaurus on the edge of the stampede. "Get down close to that one."

She felt Grappler's hesitation, her deepest instincts rising up to warn Magdalys away from this ridiculous plan.

Fubba fubba fubba, the dactyl chirped within her, a gentle precaution.

"I know, girl. Ain't nothing else to it but to do it though." Reluctantly, Grappler swooped lower until they were just above the beast's bouncing back. Magdalys patted her lovingly and then slid out of the saddle, dangling herself down from the stirrups. If she slipped, or if the dino decided to move at the last second, she'd be trampled instantly. But she couldn't think about that. She couldn't think about anything except her own churning rage and what had to be done.

She let go, her breath catching, and then felt the dino's thick flesh against her boots. One foot slipped, twisting her ankle sharply, and she found herself suddenly sitting, clinging to the T. rex's scaly back for dear life to keep from sliding to her death.

FUBBA FUBBA FUBBA! Grappler hooted from above.

"I'm okay, girl," Magdalys assured her. "I promise! Stay out of the reach of those jaws, okay?" She adjusted herself, trying to ignore the searing pain in her right ankle and the ache that was now pulsing through her left shoulder.

She had to concentrate!

Every bump and rumble rattled through her, igniting her injuries to new levels of pain, and dust covered the world.

The tyrannosaurus herd swung around a bend and then raced forward, screeching and hissing and snapping as they went.

Magdalys closed her eyes.

Tarangatrangatrangatranga the T. rexes huffed and gargled within her. She couldn't tell if it was the one she was on or a bunch of the ones nearby or all of them. She tried to cast her reach wider. The reply grew louder within her: *TARANGATRANGATRANGATRANGA.* Surely that meant more could feel her presence.

Over the rumble and din, Magdalys heard gunshots.

She glanced up. Montez and Mapper swooped in a ferocious tussle with the Sky Raider, the two dactyls clawing and squawking fiercely as smoke from their riders' guns wafted through the air around them. She couldn't make out who had the upper hand, but she had to focus.

TARANGATRANGATRANGATRANGA the herd chortled vapidly all around her. Her mount had swerved in now and dinos charged along on either side of them, some close enough to touch. Or to chomp her, she realized.

Up above, the other white dactyl zipped overhead. Was it going to help the fight? No — it was diving! She turned, followed the enemy ptero's trajectory to a spot in the stampede a ways behind her. All she saw there were the heads and backs of tyrannosauruses bouncing up and down.

What was it doing?

Concentrate, Magdalys. The memory of Lafarge's crisp accent and gravelly voice came to her like a ghost. She was trying. If he were here, they'd be able to end this together, no problem. But if he were here, he would insist she not tap into her rage, insist it would be the death of everyone she loved. He demanded ice, not fire. But Lafarge wasn't here, and fire was all Magdalys had.

She closed her eyes again, let the flame rise within her.

CHAPTER FORTY-THREE
CRASH BANG BOOM!

TARANGA!! TARANGA!! TARANGA!!! The rustle of tyrannosauruses within Magdalys slowed some, from an unending roaring drone to more of a chant, and she knew they were hers. At least, the bunch immediately surrounding her were.

That would have to do.

Up ahead, the valley opened into a relatively wide area with canyons looping off in several directions.

Perfect.

TARANGA!! TARANGA!! TARANGA!!

For all their wrath and ferocity, these dinos wanted direction. They seemed to ask her which way to go. Magdalys allowed a slight smile, then pulled more fire from within herself. The Knights would *not* have their victory today.

Break! she commanded, and a thundering mass of tyrannosauruses peeled off from the main group and burst toward one of the side corridors. Several stumbled in the sudden change of direction, and they immediately got crushed beneath the stampede in a howling, clattering mess. The one Magdalys was riding leapt over a fallen one and kept running, his unstoppable *taranga*s echoing deep within her.

They blazed down the canyon and then around a bend, coming out alongside the main stampede again. More T. rexes stumbled and were crushed near her, their howls arcing out into the sky. Her pack was still separated from the main herd though — she just had to send it off, and then peel away another group and scatter them too.

There wasn't much time, but if she could get a bigger —

Blam! Blam! Blam!

Magdalys glanced up, and even as she did, more dinos stumbled and fell around her. Something had streaked past in the corner of her eye but then she'd had to look back at where she was going. This was gonna be harder than she'd thought.

BLAM! Blood splashed up from a tyrannosaurus charging along beside her and it clattered to the ground and was enveloped in the stampede.

Was it the Sky Raider? She turned, arching her back to get a good view of the sky.

Earl Shamus Dawson Drek swooped along just above her on the back of one of the white dactyls. It must've been going back to retrieve him when she saw it earlier. He glared down at her with a furious scowl on his face and then held up his rifle.

BLAM!! BLAM!!

Another T. rex collapsed beside her. Where were Mapper and Montez? She twisted in the saddle, lifted her carbine, and let off shot after shot at Drek. Even if she didn't hit him, which she doubted she would, it would get him off her back for a moment or two.

Smoke and dust enveloped her as the dinos clattered along beside the larger herd and then merged with them again.

Drek had flown higher and was looping around for another pass. Magdalys tried to fire again and the gun just clicked — empty!

Grappler! Magdalys thought as hard as she could. *Help!*

If she couldn't end this by wrangling the stampede away bit by bit, she'd have to do it another way. And there was only one other way.

It was her or Drek.

Grappler squawked a fierce war cry and zoomed out of the sky toward her just as Drek angled his dactyl into a dive directly overhead.

Come on, girl, Magdalys thought, cracking open her carbine and shoving more slugs into it. *Come on!*

Shots rang out from above and dinos began dropping on all sides as the wet thunks of bullets finding flesh sounded around her.

Magdalys turned and shot directly overhead. Drek was still about fifty feet away and closing fast.

But Grappler was closing faster. She swung low over the T. rexes. Another shot sounded above and something wet sprayed Magdalys. Blood! She stood and ran along the back of the T. rex she'd been riding even as it pitched forward into the dirt.

Magdalys leapt.

All the rumblings and gunshots and the endless *taranga* seemed to fade as she reached out, felt gravity take her, imagined what being crushed by T. rexes would feel like, and then instead felt something swoosh against her. Grappler. She scrambled for purchase, wrapped her desperate fingers around a strap, and hauled herself onto the saddle, every inch of her throbbing.

Blam! BLAM!! More shots from Drek, who was bearing down on them with a hoarse yell, and even as Grappler swept upward and away she squealed with pain.

"No!" Magdalys yelled. Grappler had only just recovered from being shot in the Atchafalaya Swamplands, and now . . .

Something swooped past them: Drek was making a run for it. His white dactyl flapped away from the stampede.

But why? He had Magdalys on the run, wounded and struggling.

Grappler headed after them. Her wing had been clipped but it wasn't broken. Magdalys wasn't sure how far she'd be able to go though.

She glanced around. The skies were empty. Dust rose all

around them; tyrannosaurs hurtled past below. The Mexican encampment, or whatever was left of it, was only a few miles away.

Up ahead, Drek and his ptero were headed straight for a rocky embankment atop a nearby hill.

Because it didn't matter what happened with Magdalys. All he had to do was stay alive and the stampede would run right into President Juárez's army and crush them, and then the Imperials would be free to join forces with the Confederates and run roughshod across the Americas.

Drek had done everything he needed to. Now he just had to get away and keep the dinos on their course.

Rage seethed and swarmed within Magdalys as Grappler flapped in a crooked rush after Drek.

All that was left to Magdalys was to take him out.

There was no other option.

CHAPTER FORTY-FOUR
COME TO ME

GRAPPLER WAS STRUGGLING, but they weren't far behind. Magdalys steadied her carbine on her knee, flinching at the pain. She gazed down the barrel, and when Drek's mount flapped into view, she blasted once, then again.

A shrill caw tore the air, and Drek went flying as his dactyl spun into a lopsided tumble across the sky.

He landed out of sight, and the fall probably wasn't far enough to kill him.

"Swing low!" Magdalys commanded just as two shots rang out from below.

"You have to drop me off," Magdalys said. "You can't keep flying."

FUBBA! The reply was an unequivocal no.

BLAM! Another bullet sailed past. That jerk was creeping

in some bush, taking potshots. *BLAM!* This one whizzed so close it made Magdalys jump, dropping her carbine. She grunted, watching it tumble to the dusty plain below. It didn't matter much — she hardly stood a chance of winning in a shoot-out against him.

"Let me down!" Magdalys yelled. She knew the dactyl was thinking she'd never see her again once she dropped her off. And she was probably right. It didn't matter though. Well, that wasn't true, but . . . Magdalys couldn't think about that.

Fubbafubbafubba, Grappler warbled anxiously.

"I know," Magdalys said, pulling the reins forward and down, bringing them lower as she veered away from where Drek must've been hiding. "I don't have a weapon and this whole thing is a ridiculously hopeless escapade and it has been from the start. I know. And I don't care . . ."

It didn't sound very convincing.

"I still have to try."

Fubba, Grappler muttered, and it felt like a new kind of sadness opening up inside Magdalys. It was a very simple thought. A question: *Why?*

The shrubs and cactuses slid past below. Magdalys could make out the small branches and rivulets along their leaves. That was close enough.

Instead of answering, she slid off the saddle and let herself drop.

Fubbafubbafubbafoooo! Grappler called, but it didn't matter. She couldn't do anything.

The ground swung up at her faster than she'd expected, but Magdalys had enough time and foresight to lift her injured leg so she didn't land with her full weight on it. She tumbled forward and then rolled behind a shrub, watched Grappler fly off crookedly. Another shot rang out from not far ahead, but Grappler kept flying.

Everything ached.

Everything ached and Magdalys knew there was a very good chance she'd be dead soon, but maybe she could take Drek with her.

Grappler's parting question, or at least Magdalys's understanding of it, lingered like an echo: *Why?*

"Magdalys Roca!" Drek called. "Come out, come out!"

She sighed. Sweat covered her body. Pain sizzled through her ankle, throbbed from her shoulder. Every muscle felt like it was on fire. She shrugged off the ammunition belts she'd slung across her chest. Struggled out of her jacket.

"I don't have any more bullets! Come face me, silly child! We can talk this out!"

Talk this out, she scoffed to herself. He was lying, but what did it matter?

Why?

The question was alive inside her, a haunting.

There are forces more powerful than your rage, Lafarge had said.

Like what? Magdalys heard her own voice asking. *Tell me.*

"Where are you, little Roca?" Drek called. She heard his

boots crunching unevenly along the gravel. Was his leg wounded too? That tumble he took should've done *some* damage. "It's over, you know!"

Lafarge hadn't answered, not really. He'd hedged — told her to practice. But there was something he wouldn't tell her.

Why? The same sadness in her own inner voice she'd felt from Grappler, a heartbroken kind of accusation. A rippling of betrayal, loss.

"Come out and let me end this quickly!"

Old Lafarge had shaken his head. She hadn't known then, but she knew now. It wasn't just that she wouldn't have understood if she'd been told directly. It was that if she did understand, he knew she'd use it. He'd known it would arrive at this moment, and that it would be her only choice.

"Why?" she said, lurching to her feet.

About twenty feet away, Drek spun around, lifted his rifle.

Magdalys dove as the shot rang out and she landed in a heap. The bullet thwumped into the dirt inches away.

Needlessly reckless. This wouldn't work if she was dead. She just had to stay alive a little longer.

"Okay, okay! I lied, yes!" Drek yelled. "But now I really am out of bullets! See!" She heard the clunk of his rifle hitting the ground. "Now we're even, eh?"

Teach me the Gathering.

I can't.

Poor old Lafarge. He had been trying to protect her. He knew exactly what she'd end up having to use the Gathering to do.

Why?

There are forces more powerful than your rage, Magdalys.

The answer was so simple, had been there all along: love. Love was the answer to Grappler's sad goodbye question, the answer to all the questions really. Magdalys's rage had saved her life; it had gotten her this far. But it was love that fueled it, love that could close out the whole cycle. It was love that would save her friends' lives, her people.

She stood again; everything ached but the pain seemed so far away now that she knew what she had to do.

Up ahead, Drek stumbled toward her, flinching with each step. A dark stain spread along one of his pant legs. Sweat soaked his face and shirt. He was empty-handed.

Magdalys closed her eyes and bright color splotches spun circles around her. She took a step to steady herself and reached her hands to either side. She wouldn't fall.

"What are you doing, Magdalys Roca?"

Why? Because love. It had been there all along, right in front of Magdalys. The joy of her friends and her brother as they chatted in the bunks. The Squad, scattered and lost and perhaps soon to be leaderless — the way they trusted each other so quickly, they loved so easily.

David and Louis and Cymbeline and Halsey and Wolfgang and Redd and Hannibal.

Magdalys loved her people. It had been love all along that powered her. Love beneath the rage. Love beneath the sorrow.

It had been love that lit the spark of Lafarge's wrath all those years ago, and it had burned out of control and overwhelmed him.

But love was not only the spark, not only the foundation. It was the exactness too, the containment.

Lafarge didn't think she could contain it, because he hadn't been able to.

But Magdalys wasn't Lafarge. She'd lived a different life, in a very different world. And she knew how to pull with precision.

She thought of her friends and family, their laughter and passion. Their power.

And she thought of the dinos. The way they took care of her, of each other, the way they seemed to understand her without her explaining herself. The way they showed her the world. The way they came to her when she needed them most.

It was love that would see her through, right till the end, till right now.

Love would be the unstoppable spark, lighting her sorrow and rage together, and love would be the guiding force that kept her from destroying everything she cared about.

She reached out, her whole body tingling with what she'd discovered, with what was about to happen. Felt the click of connection inside her, larger than any she'd ever felt before. For a trembling moment, Drek's tenuous grip on the dinos held along with Magdalys's. She could sense his anger, his love even, and something bristling and uncontrollable: fear.

With a nod she brushed it all aside and then opened her eyes.

"What?" Drek said mockingly. He was only a few feet away now. "You're going to kill me with your bare hands, hm?"

"No," Magdalys said calmly as the ground began to rumble. "I won't have to."

Drek's eyes went wide. "You didn't!"

She smiled, ever so slightly. The shaking grew louder as the thunder of hundreds of pounding claws rose around them. "Of course I did."

Now she could make out growls and snarls and something else, very far away: a high-pitched noise just barely audible amidst all the other ruckus. Maybe . . . just maybe . . .

"Why?" Drek gasped, taking a step back, knowing it would do him no good.

Why? Magdalys had to laugh. It seemed so obvious now.

If she turned around, she would probably see the tops of those gigantic heads cresting over the hill, those gnashing teeth. And then she might lose her nerve, or have second thoughts. This way was better. Sure, she was terrified, but the truth of what would come felt somehow perfect anyway. She trembled with it, but she had made peace with it too.

"You stupid girl," Drek blathered.

"The last time someone called me that . . ." Magdalys said over the rising rumble. Then she just shook her head. "Never mind."

The stampede raced closer — any second now — but the high-pitched noise did too, an urgent kind of hooting.

Magdalys blinked. Then she recognized it.

Papeena!

She looked up just in time to see a shock of fluttering color sweep across the sky. "Hyacinth!" she yelled as many tiny sharp claws grabbed her arms and shoulders. "YAAAAAAAA AAAAAA!!!"

The tupus lifted her off the ground and into the sky. Down below, a wild rush of tyrannosaurs stampeded through where she'd just been standing.

"Wait!" Drek yelled. "Take me t —"

And that was the last the world heard of Earl Shamus Dawson Drek.

There was only one thing left to do, Magdalys realized as she sailed over the snarling, stampeding river of dinos. She still held the connection with them, had somehow kept it even through her terror and the breathtaking wonder of being swooshed up into the sky at the last second.

Love had been the spark, and now love would be the water that dampened the furious flames.

I release you, Magdalys thought as searing pain and the heavy pull of unconsciousness began to sweep over her. *I release you from all our rage and wrath, release you from our wars. Slow, slow, and disperse, and be free.*

And then everything became bright and the sun seemed to wipe away the world.

CHAPTER FORTY-FIVE
SUNRISE

"**M AGS?**"

Magdalys blinked awake. Rubbed her eyes. Someone was shoving her. Mapper. No, Montez.

Both!

She sat up. "You're alive! We're alive!"

The boys raised their eyebrows. "*You're* alive," Montez said.

"Ah! She lives!" a voice said, and then President Juárez's smiling face appeared between Mapper and Montez. "We were very worried. You did save my army, you know?"

"I did?"

Juárez chuckled. "She's so humble. There's coffee ready and arroz y frijoles heating up when you are ready to eat!" He walked off, shaking his head. "Qué chistosa."

Magdalys glanced around. The clink and clatter of

mealtime reached her along with the fresh smell of a bonfire. The Mexican Army had made camp on the top of a wide plateau overlooking the valley. They'd taken some casualties for sure, but everyone seemed to be in pretty good spirits as they huddled around in small circles, eating and talking about all that lay ahead. The Louisiana 9th wasn't far away; Reconnaissance Briggs was going on about some wild feat that may or may not have happened during the battle. Redd had joined them, Magdalys noticed with a smile, and was cracking up beside Bijoux, who still had Milo perched on one shoulder.

"These guys brought you in," Montez said, nodding at the cluster of tupus flitting around Dizz and Beans, clearly annoying them.

"Hyacinth," Magdalys said.

"Who?"

"They saved me." Magdalys sat up. "What happened?"

"The T. rexes changed course," Mapper said.

"And once the Imperial Army realized what had happened, they pulled back," Montez added.

"Back?"

"All the way back," Mapper said.

Magdalys blinked. "Like . . . to France?"

"Ha!" Montez shook his head. "Not yet. But still — they went into full retreat and holed up in Mexico City. So that's something. Which means —"

"The US Army won't have to fight a war on two fronts," Magdalys finished. "They're safe."

"For now!" Montez said.

She nodded. "Are we?"

Montez and Mapper glanced at each other.

"What is it?"

"Well, the Imperials being gone is a big help," Mapper said. "But Juárez's scouts report that something huge is coming our way from the west."

Magdalys cocked her head at him.

"We don't know what it is," Montez said. "Not yet anyway."

"Is it —"

"Not a dino, no. Some kind of machine, they think. It's still a few days out, and we don't even know what side it's on or if it'll maintain course."

"Also," Mapper said, "Banks's army finally made it to the border, and they're making their way toward us too. We're all supposed to meet up in a kind of no-man's-land area thirteen miles northeast of here, which'll allow them to not have technically made an incursion onto Mexican soil if any trouble erupts."

Magdalys rolled her eyes. "Late and obnoxiously bureaucratic. Super on brand."

"Also, also," Montez said. "There's a community of Apaches nearby, and no one is sure what they want or what they'll do, but they're well-armed."

"You didn't answer my question."

"Hm?"

"Are we safe?"

Montez and Mapper looked at each other again, each weighing the world around them. "Yes," Mapper finally said.

"For the time being," all three of them said at once.

Safety was always a fleeting thing, it seemed. When would it be over? Did a world even exist where she would know true safety? Where Magdalys could just be a kid instead of a dinowarrior, barely snatching victories from the jaws of utter destruction again and again? Maybe that world didn't exist yet, but it would one day. And she would fight to make it real — if not for herself, then for the next generation of kids. Or maybe the one after that.

However long it took, Magdalys knew what she had to do: She would fight, and she would win. Whatever it took.

A NOTE ON THE PEOPLE, PLACES & DINOS IN THE DACTYL HILL SQUAD

All together now, say it with me: **There were no dinosaurs during the Civil War era!** In fact, there were no dinosaurs at any point in time during human history. The Dactyl Hill Squad series is historical fantasy. That means it's based on an actual time and place, events that actually happened, but I also get to make up awesome stuff, like that there were dinosaurs running around. So some of the people, places, and events are based on real historical facts, some are inspired by real historical facts, and some are just totally made up. Throughout this note, I've given some recommendations on books that helped me pull all this together; some of them were written for adult readers, so make sure they're the right ones for you before diving in.

PEOPLE!

Magdalys Roca and the other orphans are not based on any specific people, but there was indeed a Colored Orphan Asylum, and their records speak of a family of kids mysteriously dropped off from Cuba without much explanation. That was part of the inspiration behind this book. You can read those stories and more about the Colored Orphan Asylum in

Leslie Harris's book *In the Shadow of Slavery: African Americans in New York City, 1626–1863.*

Cymbeline Crunk and her brother, Halsey, are inspired by Ira Aldridge and James Hewlett, two early black Shakespearean actors who performed in New York City. Hewlett cofounded the African Grove Theater, the first all-black Shakespearean troupe in the United States. Halsey and Cymbeline Crunk are entirely made-up characters. You can read more about Hewlett in Shane White's book *Stories of Freedom in Black New York* and more about Ira in *Ira's Shakespeare Dream*, by Glenda Armand and illustrated by Floyd Cooper.

General Ulysses S. Grant was the leading commander of the US Army by the end of the Civil War and went on to become president of the United States. During the war, he quickly became one of President Lincoln's favorite generals for his unwavering commitment to victory and his determination under fire. While he was never known to have an allosaurus named Samantha or a microdactyl named Giuseppe, he did spend time in New Orleans just after the fall of Vicksburg and suffered a riding accident while reviewing troops that left him bed-bound and in a cast at the Saint Charles Hotel for several days.

Both the **Louisiana 9th** and the **Louisiana Native Guard** were all-black divisions of the US Army. The Native Guard didn't fight at Milliken's Bend but were involved in a famous assault at Port Hudson. While the soldiers we meet here are entirely made up, many of their names are taken from actual soldiers who fought in those units, including Cailloux, Octave Rey, Hannibal, and Solomon.

In the case of the Louisiana Native Guard, the word *Native* refers to natives of Louisiana, not Native Americans, as Amaya at first thinks. It's unclear when the word *Native* became commonly used for Indigenous people. At this time in American history, the US Government was fighting a war of extermination against the many Indigenous nations, many of whom they'd already forced to relocate during the Trail of Tears a few decades earlier.

You can read about the Native Guard in *The Louisiana Native Guards: The Black Military Experience During the Civil War* by James G. Hollandsworth Jr.

General Ely Samuel Parker was a real-life Seneca lawyer, engineer, and diplomat. Both Harvard University and the New York Bar Association refused him entry because of his race. He eventually went on to become a key engineer and general during the Civil War and one of General Grant's right-hand men. After the war, he went on to be the first Native person to hold the position of Commissioner of Indian Affairs.

General Nathaniel Banks was one of the first "political generals" appointed by Lincoln during the Civil War. After a series of defeats on the battlefield, Banks became the commander of the Department of the Gulf, which put him in charge of New Orleans and the Mississippi River.

Rose Nicaud, also known as "Old Rose," was the first New Orleans street vendor to offer fresh coffee. She purchased her freedom and then began selling her famous baked calas and café au laits in the French Market in the early 1800s.

The famous **Café Du Monde** was founded during the Civil War — coffee shortages caused Creole chefs to mix their beans with chicory, creating the delicious blend that New Orleans has become known for. Café Du Monde was segregated for the first hundred years of its existence and didn't serve black customers until 1964, when the Civil Rights Act was passed.

Benito Juárez was a Zapotecan lawyer from the southern state of Oaxaca who became the president of Mexico in 1857. He fended off various attacks on Mexico, including by the French, and maintained his role as president even when forced to flee the capital with his cabinet. Eventually, the French were defeated and the Republic of Mexico was fully restored.

Andrew Jackson came to fame as a general during the Battle of New Orleans. As president, he presided over the forced removals of tens of thousands of Native people, including most of the Cherokee, Seminole, Choctaw, Chickasaw, and Muscogee nations, in what would become known as the Trail of Tears, resulting in many thousands of deaths.

Allan Pinkerton founded the Pinkerton National Detective Agency in 1850, and the organization went on to serve as President Lincoln's bodyguard and intelligence service during the Civil War. It later became the largest private law enforcement agency in the world, and was notorious for violently disrupting the Labor Movement.

Elizabeth Crawbell is entirely made up, though she was inspired by two real-life Confederate spies: Belle Boyd, a teenager who became a famed courier and secret agent, and the widow Rose O'Neal Greenhow, who monitored Union troop buildups and coordinated spies from her Washington, DC, residence. Both were captured by the Pinkertons. You can read more about them and two women who worked for the Union side, Emma Edmonds and Elizabeth Van Lew, in Karen Abbott's *Liar, Temptress, Soldier, Spy: Four Women Undercover in the Civil War.*

Lafarge, General Zalaka, Earl Shamus Dawson Drek, and his crimson dactyl are totally made up.

Dactyl Hill is based on a real historical neighborhood in Brooklyn called Crow Hill (modern-day Crown Heights), which, along with Weeksville and several others, became a safe haven for black New Yorkers escaping the racist violence of Manhattan. You can find out more about Weeksville at the Weeksville Historical Society and in Judith Wellman's book *Brooklyn's Promised Land.*

The **Colored Orphan Asylum** was on Fifth Avenue between Forty-Second and Forty-Third Streets in Manhattan. It was burned down in the New York Draft Riots. All the orphans except one escaped, and the organization relocated to another building.

By the second half of 1863, when this book takes place, the Union Army had just achieved two major and decisive victories after two and a half years of the Civil War. At Gettysburg, the newly promoted General Meade repelled General Lee's Army of Northern Virginia, effectively ending the Confederate invasion of Pennsylvania; and in Mississippi, General Grant sacked the fortress city of Vicksburg after a prolonged siege. Starting earlier that same year, the US government finally allowed black soldiers to be mustered into service, although they insisted on paying them significantly less than their white counterparts. From Maine to the Midwest all the way down to

Louisiana, many thousands answered the call anyway. Besides fighting valiantly in combat, they agitated successfully for equal pay, and eventually made up 10 percent of the Union Army. You can read more about the famed Massachusetts 54th and 55th regiments in *Thunder at the Gates* by Douglas R. Egerton and *Now or Never! Fifty-Fourth Massachusetts Infantry's War to End Slavery* by Ray Anthony Shepard. *A History of the Negro Troops in the War of the Rebellion, 1861–1865* is also a fascinating historical overview written twenty years after the war by a former soldier and one of the first African American historians, George Washington Williams. There are numerous other books about the Civil War, but one of the best is *Battle Cry of Freedom* by James McPherson.

The Battle of Chickamauga took place over several days (not one like it does here), just south of Chattanooga, Tennessee. While some of the details depicted are made up, a few major parts really did happen that way, including the wider strategic questions the Army of the Cumberland faced once they'd chased General Bragg's Confederate forces out of Tennessee. After a vicious back-and-forth, the near-stalemate was broken when a miscommunication on the Union side led to one regiment being moved out of the way just as the Confederates charged, which then divided the Federal forces in half and collapsed their front lines. General Thomas famously held out, covering the retreat of the other units, a feat that earned him the nickname "The Rock of Chickamauga." General Sheridan's division was cut off from the rest of the army during the rout, and then regrouped and made their way back to try to reinforce Thomas as night was falling, although it's unclear how much help they were able to provide.

The Battle of Milliken's Bend, which Montez was wounded in, was indeed an important moment in the victory at Vicksburg, as the 9th Louisiana Regiment of African Descent and others repelled an attempt by the Confederates to reinforce their besieged troops.

The **Knights of the Golden Circle** were composed of various pro-slavery advocates throughout the Americas who were dedicated to bringing an expansion of the slave states into the Caribbean and Central and South America that they dubbed "the Golden Circle."

Federal naval forces led by General Farragut took over **New Orleans** very early on in the war and the city remained in Union control the whole time. A city known for delicious food and a mix of cultures, New Orleans is considered the birthplace of jazz, which grew in part out of the second-line funeral tradition that Hannibal tells Magdalys about.

The **Mardi Gras Indians** are a New Orleans cultural tradition dating back to the nineteenth century, when black Americans wanted to honor the Native Americans who had helped them out during slavery. To this day, the different Krewes create brightly colored, feather-adorned regalia and parade through the streets of New Orleans on certain days of the year.

The Franco–Mexican War took place between 1861 and 1867. Conservative Mexican leaders sought help from imperial European powers when they were defeated in a democratic election by the left-leaning reformer Benito Juárez. The French sent troops and promised Mexico to the Austrian Archduke Maximilian. (In this book, he's already there; in reality he didn't arrive till 1864. The dinos got him across the ocean faster!) The Mexican army initially had success, repulsing the imperial advance on the city of Puebla in May 1863. (The holiday Cinco de Mayo is a commemoration of that victory!) But the imperial forces rallied and pushed through, conquering a succession of cities and then the capital, which sent President Juárez and his soldiers scattering. They kept fighting though, and eventually Juárez and his generals defeated the French and executed Maximilian.

The Battle of New Orleans was part of the War of 1812, but it didn't happen in New Orleans or 1812! In fact, it took place in the nearby town of Chalmette. The battle played out much like Lafarge describes (minus the dinos), and was a stunning defeat for the British.

For more information on the Native people and history of this era, please see *An Indigenous Peoples' History of the United States for Young People* by Roxanne Dunbar-Ortiz, adapted by Jean Mendoza and Debbie Reese.

DINOS, PTEROS & OTHER ASSORTED -SAURIA

Of course, a lot less is known about dinosaurs than about Civil War–era United States. Because of this, and because this is a fantasy novel, I took more liberties with the creation of the dinosaurs in this story than I did with the history. Experts can make intelligent guesses based on the fossil data, but we don't really know exactly what prehistoric animals looked like, smelled like, or how they acted. In the world of Dactyl Hill Squad, the dinos never went extinct, but humans did subdue and domesticate them as beasts of burden and war.

The **tyrannosaurus rex** is probably the most famous of the dinosaurs. It lived during the late Cretaceous Period and was known as the king of dinos. They were bipedal (meaning they walked on two feet), carnivorous (meaning they ate meat), and about as long as a school bus.

The **brachiosaurus** was a humongous herbivorous (meaning it ate plants) quadruped (meaning it walked on four legs). Its long neck allowed it to eat leaves from the tallest trees. It lived during the Late Jurassic Period and probably didn't hoot the way the ones in the Dactyl Hill world do.

Sauropod is a general term for the gigantic quadrupedal dinosaurs with long necks, long tails, and relatively small heads. In the Dactyl Hill Squad world, they are used for transportation, cargo carrying, and construction.

As Magdalys points out, **pterodactyls** weren't dinosaurs, they were pterosaurs, flying reptiles closely related to birds. They flew through Jurassic-era skies munching on insects, fish, and small reptiles. Generally about the size of seagulls, they weren't really large enough to carry a person. A group of pterodactyls is not called a squad (although maybe it should be!) and scientists don't suspect them to have been pack dependent as described in the book. But who knows?

Raptors were a group of very intelligent, bipedal carnivores. They had rod-straight tails and a giant claw on each foot, and they hunted in packs during the Late Cretaceous Period.

Triceratopses were herbivorous quadrupeds about the size of an ice cream truck that roamed the earth during the Late Cretaceous Period. They had three horns: one protruding from the snout and two longer ones that stuck out from a wide shield over their eyes that stretched out over their neck.

The **diplodocus** was one of the longest known sauropods and it roamed the North American plains toward the end of the Jurassic Period. It was over ninety feet long! Basically the size of a nine-story building turned on its side.

Pteranodons were large, mostly toothless pterosaurs without long tails. In fact, their name means "toothless lizard." Quetzalcoatlus, the largest of pterosaurs, was big as a fighter plane — forty-five feet long. They ruled the skies of the Late Cretaceous Period.

Archaeopteryx, which means "Old Wing," are considered to be the oldest form of bird. About the size of a raven, these Jurassic-era dinosaurs had sharp teeth, a long bony tail, and hyperextensible second toes called "killing claws." Yikes!

Sinornithosaurs were Cretaceous Period birdlike dinos once believed to have a venomous bite, although experts now don't believe that to be the case. They glided and hunted through the skies of what we now call China, and their name means "Chinese bird lizard."

The **parasaurolophuses** were Late Cretaceous Period plant eaters that walked on both four and two legs. They had a long bony crest that extended from the backs of their heads.

Dimetrodons, also known as finbacks, were short, four-legged synapsids (creatures that roamed the earth forty million years *before* the dinosaurs) that were recognizable for the tall sails protruding from their spines. They are related to modern mammals.

Spinosauruses were large theropods that hunted the wetland areas of the Cretaceous Period. They had long, crocodile-like snouts, and the bony spines extending from their vertebrae were probably connected by skin to give a sail-like look.

The name **tupuxuara** is a reference to a type of familial spirit of the Tupi people of the Brazilian Amazon. Although the ones we meet in this book are very small, the tupus were actually large pterosaurs that roamed the South American skies of the Early Cretaceous Period.

The **gallimimus** was a long legged theropod dino that lived during the Late Cretaceous. They used their tail to balance themselves as they ran and are believed to be one of the fastest land dinosaurs.

The **scutosaur,** whose name means "shield lizard," was not a dinosaur, but rather a large, four-legged parareptile with an armored hide.

A NOTE ON WEAPONS

In this messy, broken time of mass shootings and state violence, it's important to note that guns almost always create more problems than they solve. More than that: Young people suffer with trauma from those problems in increasing and heartbreaking numbers. This is an adventure story, and it takes place during a war, in an era when folks were being kidnapped and sold into slavery and an invading rebel army threatened the nation's capital. Guns are one of the parts of life in that time that I chose to include in this story, but I hope that a) the dangers, both physical and emotional, of gun violence ring loud and clear on the page, and b) we one day live in a time when gun violence doesn't exist anymore at all.

Rifled muskets are enhanced versions of the old Revolutionary War firearms. The rifled muzzles gave these weapons greater precision, and their caplock mechanisms made them easier to load and fire than their flintlock ancestors. Rifled muskets, both Enfields and Springfields, were the most commonly issued guns on both sides of the Civil War.

Many rifled muskets were armed with a **bayonet**, a sharpened sword attached to the muzzle that could be used to stab an attacker.

The **carbine** is smaller and lighter than the rifled musket, with a shorter barrel. Because they are breach-loading, meaning you insert the bullets at the middle of the gun instead of into the muzzle, they are easier to shoot from horseback (or dinoback) and thus were favored by cavalry (mounted) units.

The **Gatling** is a multibarreled rapid-fire gun invented by Richard Gatling, a North Carolinian who, horrified that more soldiers died of disease than from combat during warfare, decided to invent a weapon that would "supersede the necessity of large armies." Which doesn't totally make that much sense and definitely didn't work out that way, but hey . . . He sold his new weapon exclusively to the US Army, but it didn't see too much action during the Civil War as it had only just been invented.

The **howitzer** is a short-barreled smoothbore mobile artillery cannon that could fire shells of twelve, twenty-four, and thirty-two pounds in a high trajectory. They were used as defensive weapons and to flush enemies out of their entrenched hiding places.

ACKNOWLEDGMENTS

Thank you to superstar editors Nick Thomas and Jody Corbett!

Thank you to the whole team at Scholastic, who have been amazing throughout this process, especially Melissa Schirmer; Erin Berger; Amy Goppert; Lizette Serrano; Emily Heddleson; Erik Ryle; Rachel Feld; Shannon Pender; and Gavin Brown, Erika Scipione, and Fay Koh, who created the online Dactyl Hill Squad game, *Rescue Run*. It! Is! So! Awesome! Check it out at: kids.scholastic.com/kids/books/dactyl-hill-squad/.

Nilah Magruder always brings such vivid life to Magdalys and her friends, and it takes my breath away each time I get to see a new image of hers. Thank you, Nilah! And a huge thank-you to Afu Chan for the terrific Dactyl Hill Squad logo and to Christopher Stengel for bringing it all together with such grace and precision.

To Eddie Schneider and Joshua Bilmes and the whole team at JABberwocky Lit: You are wonderful. Thank you.

Many thanks to Leslie Shipman at The Shipman Agency and Lia Chan at ICM.

Dr. Debbie Reese was once again terrifically generous with her time and wisdom and analysis. She gave detailed notes, and I'm deeply grateful. Her work at American Indians in Children's Lit is always a crucial resource and necessary reading.

I was talking through some scenes with Jalisa Roberts and Brittany Nicole Williams one day. Brittany wondered if Café Du Monde had even been integrated yet back then — turns out it hadn't and wouldn't be for another hundred years — and Jalisa told me about Rose Nicaud, the original coffee seller of the French Market. Many thanks to both of them for those insights and all their help along the way!

Thanks to the brilliant writer, scholar, and friend David Bowles for his thoughts on the Mexico scenes and language.

Thanks to Dr. Laura Kelley! All incorrect historical or dinofactual matter is my own fault, and it's probably on purpose, unless it's in the back matter, and then it's totally my bad.

Thanks always to my amazing family, Brittany, Dora, Marc, Malka, Lou, Calyx, and Paz. Thanks to Iya Lisa and Iya Ramona and Iyalocha Tima, Patrice, Emani, Darrell, April, and my whole Ile Omi Toki family for their support; also thanks to Oba Nelson "Poppy" Rodriguez, Baba Malik, Mama Akissi, Mama Joan, Tina, and Jud, and all the wonderful folks of Ile Ase. Thanks also to Sam, Sorahya, Akwaeke, and Lauren.

Baba Craig Ramos: We miss you and love you and carry you with us everywhere we go. Rest easy, Tío. Ibae bayen tonu.

I give thanks to all those who came before us and lit the way. I give thanks to all my ancestors; to Yemonja, Mother of Waters; gbogbo Orisa, and Olodumare.

ABOUT THE AUTHOR

Daniel José Older has always loved monsters, whether historical, prehistorical, or imaginary. He is the *New York Times* bestselling author of numerous books for readers of all ages: for middle grade, the Dactyl Hill Squad series, the first book of which was named a New York Times Notable Book and to the NPR and Washington Post Best Books of the Year lists, and the second of which was named a Publishers Weekly Best of Summer Reading; for young adults, the acclaimed Shadowshaper Cypher, winner of the International Latino Book Award; and for adults, *Star Wars: Last Shot*, the Bone Street Rumba urban fantasy series, and *The Book of Lost Saints*. He has worked as a bike messenger, a waiter, and a teacher, and was a New York City paramedic for ten years. Daniel splits his time between Brooklyn and New Orleans.

You can find out more about him at danieljoseolder.net.

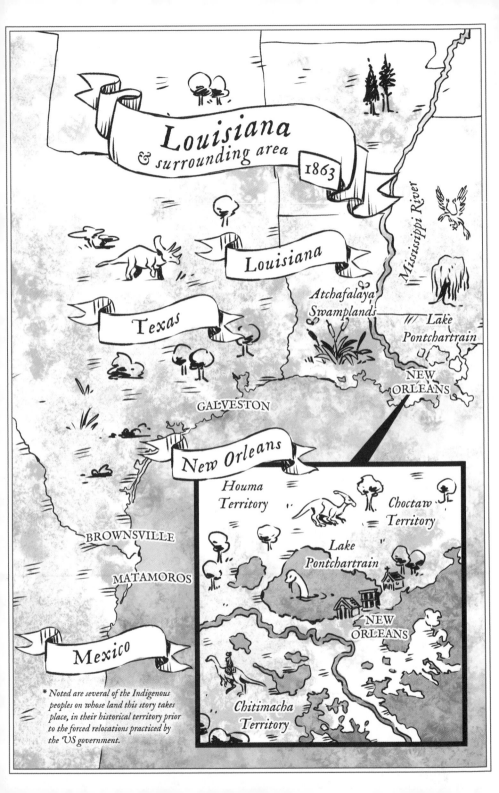